C000051736

Better

Than

Biscuits

Phoenix Writing Group

Published by Phoenix Writing Group

©Phoenix Writing Group 2021

This book is copyright.
Subject to statutory exception and to provisions of relevant
collective licensing agreements, no part of this publication
may be reproduced without the prior written permission of
the author(s).

It is a work of fiction.
The characters, places and events are the product of each
author's imagination or are used fictitiously.
Any resemblance to actual persons, living or dead,
is purely coincidental.

ISBN 978-0-9934063-3-1

Edited by Kim Kimber
(www.kimkimber.co.uk)

With thanks to Trisha Todd and Sue Duggans
for their help with proofreading

Cover design: With thanks to Katie Sibbons

50% of the proceeds from this anthology are being donated
to Southend in Sight – the Community Services Division of
Southend Blind Welfare Organisation.
(Registered Charity no. 1069765)

Contents

Introduction

They say that time goes by quickly when you're having fun and that's certainly been the case with our writing group. Nearly ten years have passed since we first formed, during which time friendships have been forged, tea drunk and biscuits dunked while we've honed our craft. This monthly ritual has given rise to the title of our latest anthology; *Better Than Biscuits*.

All our experiences, good and bad, are reflected in our stories, and we couldn't live through a global pandemic without it impacting our writing so that gets a mention too, although that's not our main focus, and you will find a mix of genres and styles within these pages. Ghost stories sit beside heart-warming tales and historical writing, and there is also a touch of fantasy, mystery and romance, not to mention the occasional poem.

We were originally known as WoSWI Writing Group and we published three anthologies under this name: *Write on the Coast*, the award-winning *Ten Minute Tales* and *A Book For All Seasons*. Two years ago, we underwent some changes and emerged as Phoenix Writing Group and all the stories and poems in this book have been written since then.

As always, we not only hope to entertain but to do some good with our writing, and 50% of the royalties from this book will be going to help support a local charity, Southend in Sight (please turn to page 181 for more information).

A huge thank you to everyone who has supported us on our journey and bought our previous books. It means a great deal to us and has raised money for some good causes.

We hope you enjoy our first anthology as Phoenix Writing Group. Who knows what we might achieve in the next ten years!

The Phoenix Birds

Barbara Sleap

The Phoenix ladies from the ashes arose
Pens in hand to write stories and prose.
Each has a genre, maybe romance or horror,
To make readers cry or get hot under the collar.

Lois, Kim, Trisha, Pat and Michele
Babs and Sue all have tales to tell.
The Thursday meetings with biscuits and tea
Often hilarious, we're good friends you see.

Characters created by Lois and Sue;
Some quirky, some sad, but they always ring true.
Sci-fi from Pat, who likes the unknown,
Michele's so descriptive, nature's her zone.

Trisha's stories are witty and you might get the gist
Then the unexpected happens as they end with a twist.
Read Babs' stories if you get the chance
But only if you fancy a little taste of France.

Kim runs the group, she writes like a pro
And helps with our grammar to make our words flow
But we still make mistakes, well just now and then,
That's when she's ready with her trusty red pen.

We're proud of our books but don't like to boast;
Ten Minute Tales and *Write on the Coast*
A Book for all Seasons, and there will be more
We're about to publish book number four.

Mind the Gap

Sue Duggans

It started with the grating and screeching of metal on metal then the chilling thud which pulsated through the length of the tube train. Standing passengers were flung forward landing in chaos on the floor. Then there was darkness and terrified screams. The panic was palpable.

Caroline fell onto Elsa who whimpered quietly. She spoke reassuringly and, trembling, held her close. After the initial commotion an eerie silence fell, followed by muted voices. Caroline was troubled by single words which she could make out through the alarm and confusion – 'bomb… crash…suicide'. Her heart pounded.

Less than fifteen minutes earlier, Caroline and Elsa had boarded the train and been lucky enough to find a seat. At this time in the morning the Tube was always tightly packed with commuters. Caroline stroked Elsa's soft head. Her fingers traced the contours of her face and ears and she sensed her breath. It had been just over three months since the last visit to the consultant and Caroline was anxious. Elsa seemed oblivious but maybe sensed Caroline's unease.

'The next stop is Moorgate…mind the gap…' At the station people shuffled off and more crowded on, jostling for a small space. Elsa's eyes darted warily from person to person.

In the crowd to her right, Caroline detected someone wearing Simon's favourite aftershave, Ralph Lauren's Polo Double Black, which was instantly recognisable. Simon had worn it on their wedding day and on the day that Elsa arrived in their lives. She could pick out the masculine, woody tones above all other scents and odours which filled the oppressive, warm air. She thought about the smoothness of the sleek glass bottle with its little embossed logo and thought of Simon.

'The next stop is Old Street…mind the gap…' This was their stop. Caroline got up and, with a firm hold on Elsa, manoeuvred her way to the door. That's when it had happened, without warning, shaking every passenger to the very core.

People began to untangle themselves from each other and, in the diminishing darkness, collect their scattered belongings. It appeared, unbelievably, that injuries were few but kindness and compassion one for the other was plentiful. The tannoy system had kicked in. The voice urged passengers to keep calm and remain where they were despite the dark and the heat. The dark didn't worry Caroline but the heat was unbearable. The train had collided with one which was stationary and it was anticipated that the engine could limp into Old Street within minutes.

Shortly afterwards the train jolted into motion and, very slowly, pulled into the station. When the carriage doors opened, a number of authoritative voices could be heard giving direction and reassurance to passengers.

'Can we let the lady with the guide dog off first please?'

Caroline stepped off the train and Elsa's tail wagged vigorously, sensing safety. Caroline stroked her head and smiled.

Elsie's List

Kim Kimber

Gran is snoozing in the chair, her head lolling on her chest, her breathing deep and even. My hand is cramping from holding hers but when I attempt to pull away to stretch out my fingers, she squeezes more tightly.

The care home is clean and efficient but still carries a faint smell of steamed fish and cabbage. The TV is on but no one is watching.

I glance at the clock, my mind wandering to this evening's gathering. Nat is going to be there and I want to be home in time to have a shower. Idly, I wonder what to wear. My phone beeps and I pick it up with my free hand.

'I'm going to kill the traitor.' Elsie's voice is surprisingly strong as she shouts across the room. I lower my head, suddenly fascinated by the image of a LOLcat on my phone screen.

'That's right, I'm going to kill him; he's on my list.'

'Be quiet, Elsie, you're upsetting the other residents,' a young carer, Lena, says in a firm voice.

'I'll kill you too, if you try to stop me,' says Elsie. 'I can you know; I've been trained by the SOE.'

I swallow a giggle.

'I'll get him, don't you worry. I'm trained in combat.'

I glance up as Elsie bends forward and retrieves a long-handled comb from down the side of her slipper. She points it towards the window. 'C'est un *traître*.'

It's 1944 and Yvette is in German-occupied France. Her mission is to help the resistance identify Nazi sympathisers and take them out of circulation. She's sitting outside a German-run café along the Champs Élysées waiting for her mark to appear so she can follow him. A swastika hangs above the door of this popular Third Reich coffee house and the air crackles with the harsh, guttural sounds of the German accent. Yvette retrieves a cigarette from the packet of Gauloises on the table and puts it to her lips. This particular café is popular with high-ranking officers and one of them strikes a match and offers her a light. Yvette smiles and nods but avoids eye contact. The officer lingers...

Lena makes her way over. Close to, she doesn't look much older than me and I am immediately grateful for my comfortable office job.

'Don't mind Elsie,' she says. 'She's harmless enough. It's the dementia. She thinks she's a spy.'

'Oh...' I start to form a response along the lines that dementia sufferers often forget their more recent past although they don't generally invent previous lives, but I think better of it.

Instead I say, 'Who does she want to kill?'

'Pierre, the new resident. He's got some of the ladies quite excited. I think it's the French accent.' Lena nods towards the garden where a distinguished-looking gentleman with salt and pepper hair is ringed by a group of women, arthritic knees and incontinent bladders momentarily forgotten. 'Elsie thinks he's on her hit list, bless her. I don't know how she's got the energy at her age. She received her card from the Queen a couple of years back.'

Yvette is aware of the officer hovering near her table but doesn't react.

'Are you alone, Fraulein?'

She takes a puff of her cigarette and pretends not to understand. The officer steps closer. 'Fraulein?' He touches her on the shoulder and she looks up. She is young and pretty and the officer smiles appreciatively 'Wie hiessen sie?'

She shrugs her shoulders so the officer points to himself and says, 'Karl.'

'Yvette.' This name is now as familiar to her as her own.

He reaches over and tucks a stray curl of hair behind her ear. It is an intimate gesture and she shudders somewhere deep inside. At that moment, there is a commotion a few doors down and a man is dragged out into the street by the Gestapo. The officer tips his cap at her and takes a few steps forward to watch as the man is executed in front of his family. Yvette hastily throws some coins on the table, picks up her cigarettes and slips away unnoticed. She will not return to that café.

'Is Elsie ranting on again?' I nod and smile at Ada, who sits next to Gran.

'Take no notice.' She leans over and pats my hand. I like Ada. She was an archaeologist and has been on digs all over the world. She always has interesting stories to tell.

It's true what Mum says, the care home is a great leveller. Lawyers and doctors sit next to cleaners and bus drivers. Gran was a stage actress, and a fairly good one I believe...though you wouldn't think so now. She can hardly remember her name, let alone all those lines.

'Horrible to lose your mind,' Ada continues. 'I'm one of the lucky ones; wouldn't be in here if it wasn't for that fall, but they take good care of us.'

Ada is tipped back in the recliner, her legs covered by a blanket. Everything she needs is within reach: glass of juice, glasses, tissues and a pot for her false teeth. Still, I wouldn't describe her situation as 'lucky'.

Across the room, Elsie watches.

Yvette is one of a small number of female spies drafted into France as, one by one, her male counterparts have been discovered, tortured and killed. A change of direction was needed and who would suspect an attractive young woman? But Yvette was not selected for her looks, lovely though she is, she was chosen for her aptitude with languages and ability to remain calm under pressure. Her unflappable demeanour is essential to the job. The dangers are real and ever-present.

I am getting ready to leave, wondering what to wear that evening, when Pierre comes in from the garden. He stands tall, with a straight back, for a man of advanced years.

He retreats to his armchair in the corner of the room farthest away from Elsie, before his entourage has time to follow. He picks up a book from the table and holds it in front of his face. It's in English, by an American author, and I'm not certain if he's reading it or using it as camouflage. But Elsie has seen him and is on her feet advancing towards him, her Zimmer frame scraping across the laminated floor. She moves fast and, before Lena can intercept, she comes to a halt in front of Pierre.

Yvette crouches under the bridge, hoping she can't be seen from the road and that her bicycle, hidden from view behind the front wall of the farmhouse, won't be discovered and give her away.

One of the Germans walks onto the bridge, the sound of heavy boots pausing directly above her head. He strikes a match. She can smell tobacco. He stands above her smoking. Yvette hardly dares breathe.

A cigarette butt is thrown over the bridge into the water. The boots retrace their steps and Yvette exhales. She hears the clunking of car doors. They're leaving. She stays put for a few minutes to make sure the patrol car doesn't return before crawling out of her hiding place and brushing the mud off her skirt. Inside the farmhouse the maquisards are holding a local man captive. Yvette has had him under surveillance for some time for passing information to the

Germans. She removes the garrotte wire from under the baguettes in her bicycle panier and walks towards the farmhouse.

Elsie is talking to Pierre in what sounds like fluent French. The effortless tumble of words would be impressive from a much younger person but coming from Elsie it is nothing short of remarkable. Her voice sounds more lyrical in another language, as if she has taken on a completely different persona.

Lena appears beside me. 'Any idea what they're on about?' she asks, hopefully.

I shake my head. 'They're speaking French but it's too fast for me,' I say wishing I'd paid more attention in GCSE French.

'I should get Elsie back to her seat,' says Lena, 'before it gets messy.'

On the way back to central Paris, Yvette's bike gets a puncture. She is at the roadside, bike upside down, trying to fix it when a patrol car rolls past. The car slows and then comes to a halt a short distance ahead. Yvette curses under her breath as one of the two occupants alights from the car and strides towards her.

'Kann ich dir helfen, Fraulein?'

Yvette does not reply.

'I said, can I help you?' The German speaks to her in her native tongue but she shows no recognition and continues trying to mend her puncture. She knows it is hopeless as the

wheel buckled when she hit a rut in the uneven road, tipping her off and rendering her means of escape useless. The officer pushes her aside, looks at the bike and tuts. He then lifts it up and carries it towards the car, beckoning her to follow.

Yvette carefully picks up the panier, which she has removed from the bike to mend the puncture, and rearranges the contents before walking after him.

The officer puts her bike in the rear of the car and gestures for her to get in.

'Merci, monsieur,' she manages to say, climbing in alongside her bike.

He gets in the driver's seat, next to the other occupant, a young male officer. The two talk and joke together in German about what they might do with their rescued damsel. Yvette's face remains impassive.

There is something familiar about the man behind the wheel, who keeps glancing back at her in the rear-view mirror. She recognises his voice. Yvette is good with voices and can distinguish between different regional accents in French and German, as well as her mother tongue. It helps to keep her safe. It is the officer from the café on the Champs Èlysées.

Yvette averts her gaze, glad her unruly auburn hair is today covered by a scarf. The journey feels long but, eventually, the car rumbles into the outskirts of Paris. The car pulls up outside a velo repair shop and the driver gets out and lifts her bike onto the pavement.

'Merci,' she says, jumping out behind him.

She takes the handlebars and starts to wheel the damaged bicycle inside the shop but the German puts a restraining hand on her arm.

'Halt!'

He turns her face towards him and tips her head up, before removing a clean handkerchief from his pocket and dabbing at her face. 'Du bist verletzt.'

She does not respond.

He shows her the blood-stained handkerchief and touches her cheek and she nods in understanding. 'Merci.'

The officer gets back into the car and his colleague slaps him on the back, laughs and says something obscene. Yvette enters the shop, her legs shaking. The blood is not hers, but that of the traitor who was tortured and killed back at the farmhouse.

Lena lightly touches Elsie's arm. The centenarian spins around, as if ready to retaliate. It takes a moment for the past to catch up with the present, the intervening years lost in time. But Elsie realises where she is and shuffles uncomplainingly back to her chair.

I kiss Gran on the cheek, say goodbye to Ada and wave at Lena, my thoughts now fully occupied with the evening ahead.

The boy is young, around fifteen or sixteen, but Yvette has no sympathy for him. He is a collaborator, regardless of his age, caught feeding information about the resistance to the Nazis. He is being held between two French freedom

16

fighters.

'Traître,' she says, and spits in his bloodied and bruised face.

The boy's legs give out and a damp patch appears on his trousers. They have been following the lad for some time, tracking his movements, observing as he slips notes to the Germans, condemning his countrymen. The worst kind of betrayal. There will be no mercy...

The next day is Sunday and I am in bed, thinking about the previous night, when Mum knocks on the door and then appears holding a cup of tea.

'Sorry, love,' she says. 'I know it's early, but I'm going to the care home.'

I sit up quickly. 'Is Gran okay?'

'Yes, she's fine, but one of the residents has died.'

'Oh no, that's sad, which one?' I ask, hoping it isn't Ada.

'It's Pierre. They found him this morning. He was very popular although he hasn't been there long, so it's come as a bit of a shock to them all. I don't think Gran will know much about it but I want to check on her.'

'Do they know how he died?'

'I don't think so. He was old, but it's still a bit sudden and unexpected.'

An image of Elsie comes into my mind. I shake my head and smile.

It is quickly over and the boy drops to the ground, his body lifeless. Another threat has been neutralised. Now to find his accomplice, Pierre. He may try to hide but Yvette will find him. She prides herself on tracking down everyone on her list, no matter how long it might take.

The Cell

Michele Hawkins

Susie slowly opened her eyes, one at a time. Lying flat on her back, it took a minute for her eyes to adjust to the gloom as she gingerly turned her head from left to right trying to work out where she was. All she could see was a bricked ceiling and walls surrounding her. She became aware of a painful throbbing in her head as if she had hit it quite hard. Lifting her right hand up she examined her scalp, gently pressing down and then checking her fingers for blood. None found, thank goodness!

Carefully she hauled herself up to a sitting position, stretching and flexing each leg and foot in turn. Rolling her left ankle, she noticed some discomfort but concluded it was no more than a strain. A tiny light caught her attention. Swaying first one way then the other it appeared to be dancing. Susie held her breath as she fixated on the light. All of a sudden, there were lots of tiny lights all around her, spinning and swooping, moving faster and faster until, with a whoosh, they disappeared. *Fireflies*, thought Susie, *but what are they doing here and where is here*?

Turning over onto all fours she rose unsteadily but, unable to stand fully upright, she shuffled forward, hands outstretched towards the nearest wall. Feeling her way along she moved slowly until she came to a door. It was wooden, topped with smooth metal studs with a central metal grill. As her fingers traced the outline she came to a large metal ring. Tugging up and down she tried to release the latch but nothing happened. Frantic now, she banged on the door with both fists, shouting as loudly as she could but to no avail. Dejected, she slumped down the wall to a seated position on the floor and wept. She felt confused, scared and cold.

After a while, Susie pulled herself out of her stupor and resumed her exploration of the room. Her foot nudged something and, bending down, she discovered a mattress covered in a thin blanket which she grabbed and gratefully wrapped herself in. Sitting down she spied a tray just to her left perched on a small table. Realising just how hungry and thirsty she was, she cautiously lifted a cup to her lips and took a sip. It appeared to be simply water and so she gulped it down. Wiping her mouth with the back of her hand she paused before tucking into a sandwich. *Odd*, she thought, *strawberry jam and banana.* Nonetheless she greedily devoured it.

***

Twenty miles away in Woodham Police Station the morning chatter hushed as the boss entered the room to brief his team on the latest abduction in the area. This was the third girl in as many years and the youngest yet. Susie Matthews was thirteen and had been on her way home from school when she disappeared.

To date, none of the girls had been found.

Wendy Wet-Leg

Lois Maulkin

And you are home from work, at last. Today has been so very hot. The hottest day of the hottest summer there has ever been and you and he have been living together for just a few weeks. Being with him, well, it is a joy, all you have wanted. It is so hot, you can think of nothing but how you long to be in cool water. You daydream of the sea as you walk up from the station.

'Are you hungry?' you say, looking listlessly into the fridge. He says he isn't, it's too hot to eat. You make cups of tea and say, 'Let's go for a swim.'

You know it is a big deal for him. As a boy, he'd loved swimming, lived in the water. Won competitions. There is a childhood photo of him from the local paper. He is standing with David Wilkie at the edge of the swimming pool holding up a medal, proud, smiling the crinkle-eyed smile you love, his fringe hanging damp across his thin face. It would have been taken a year or so before his cancer struck. He had been a year in hospital following a knock to his left shin, when he fell from his bike, which didn't heal…didn't heal…didn't heal. He has told you of the chemotherapy, the radiotherapy, the sickness, the loneliness and the endless books he read. Your heart ached for him: the sick, frightened little boy whose mother had visited only now and again. He has told you how, ten years later, a drunk driver had knocked him off his motorbike and smeared him across the road. They'd sent the air ambulance away as he was dead at the scene so they'd said, but he'd survived, miraculously, his right side cobbled back together. A medical marvel.

He had to learn to walk again. And he has told you of the time, ten years later still, when he'd been hanging out the washing and had heard his shin bone snap. Bones don't take kindly to massive radiation, it turns out. There was another wound on his shin that would not heal, infection that would not clear, and the awful decision that, to save his life again, his lower leg would have to be cut away. He was given a below-the-knee prosthetic. That was fifteen, sixteen years ago and he has not been swimming since. You know he hates his body. He hates anyone to see it. He hates the metal rods in his arm, the hand he cannot open, the patchwork skin grafts, scars, his mended legs, the foot that isn't there. He hates being three inches shorter than he used to be.

It is new to you, to love the way you love him. You love the long leanness of him, the paleness, the sharp hip bones and what fizzes between you as your skin touches his, peaceful and exciting at the same time. You love his vulnerability and the cloak of barbed bravado he wears to conceal it. And the smell of him; toffee and coriander and butter, it is like a drug to you. For the first months you were together he undressed discreetly, secretly, at the side of the bed and slid in, not letting you see him. No one saw him, he told you, no one had seen him since the nurses. He would not let you scrub his back in the bath when you called through the bathroom door to offer. In case you saw.

On winter nights, cold in the cotton sheets, he'd keep his leg away from you. Then one night, the two of you curled together and, drowsing on the edge of sleep, you'd pulled his leg in to tuck his knee between your thighs.

'But, that's…is that all right?' he'd asked.

'Needs warming up,' you had murmured, 'little frozen lamb shank.' You'd heard him chuckle softly. He'd let you see it, after that. He was apologetic. You knew that to him it was abhorrent, horrific, the stuff of nightmares, to look down where his leg and foot should be and see nothing there but to you it isn't like that. It's just the way he is, his history. And, besides, there are no mangled tatters of bleeding flesh, no grizzled, withered gnarliness. Just a neat bottlenose shape, tidy skin, nothing in itself offensive in any way.

'It looks fine,' you'd said. 'Just like a leg looks when it's had that operation.'

His prosthetic leg was hot to wear, held on by big elastic sleeves. Sometimes it rubbed sores on his knee and the remaining part of his lower leg. Without it, he was dependent on crutches. It was made to be the same weight as the part of the limb that was missing, to make it feel real and keep the wearer's movement natural. It was a godsend. It was metal with valves and a ball joint ankle. But it could not get wet.

'So,' you say, holding your hair away from your sticky neck, 'shall we finish our tea and then go to the beach?'

He half smiles, but doesn't answer. It is evening but still as hot as midday.

You talk about how lovely it will be, bobbing about in the water. He says nothing, but you can tell he wants to. You pause a moment then, 'We'll be all cool. It's shallow for miles out, really safe. You love to swim.'

'It's different now,' he says. 'I don't know...'

You want to say, 'I'll hold your hand, I promise I won't let anything bad happen to you. I promise no one will stare,' but you don't because you can't make those promises and he isn't a child. So much of this relationship is about what you don't say.

You are two tuning forks singing the same note, you know each other's mind and you know he wants to go.

He drains his cup and says, 'Okay then.'

Upstairs you put on your swimming costume with a short cotton dress over the top, and he finds and puts on his old swimming trunks.

'And here's Wendy,' you say, pulling something out from under the bed.

'Who?' he asks.

'Wendy Wet-Leg,' you say, holding her up triumphantly.

It is the limb he was given to use in water, which he has only ever worn for clearing weeds from his garden pond. It is plastic, hollow, all one piece. There are two small holes, top and bottom, to let air and water in and out. Looking at them flashes you back to Sunday teatimes in your childhood, milk being poured from a blue and white can onto your bowl of fruit, someone explaining the need for the two holes, that milk won't come out unless air can go in. The ankle does not move. It is like a doll's leg. Rigid. Pink. He sits on the edge of the bed to put it on. You'd spent a lot of time on the beach before you'd moved in together. On weekends at his house, you'd often walk there on winter Sunday afternoons, bundled up in jumpers and gloves and woolly hats, ears and faces freezing. He had picked up bits of blue and green sea glass for you, smooth fragments of smashed old plates, flowery ones, bits of clay pipe. Your coat pockets always held these little beach gifts. You'd walked hand in hand along the wet shingle, dodging the waves and the icy spray, sometimes talking, sometimes not. It was a place you were happy together.

It is a cool, ten-minute journey in the air-conditioned car and the heat is an assault as you get out and cross the grass to the beach. The sun is low now. There is only a handful of people on the sand and they trail the scent of sun cream, forming long shadows that look like primitive paintings. They are dressing small children, shaking out towels, getting ready to head home for the evening. You realise they will be gone in five minutes or so and the two of you will have the beach to yourselves. It is a relief.

The water glitters in the heat and you can smell it calling you as you slip off your dress and sandals, not watching as he takes off his shirt and shorts and trainers. You don't want to make him feel more uncomfortable than he already does, or let him know you're ever so slightly nervous about how this is going to go.

You leave your clothes in a pile on the sand and walk together to the edge of the water. With your shoes off, the stones are sharp on your soles and the two of you hobble and wince comically, giggling. You look at his thin, pale torso, like a young boy's. You are thrilled he is doing this.

The air is hot even here, at the beach. There is no wind and the sea is a gently moving stillness. The tide is pulling itself up, languidly, to its highest point before pausing, holding its breath, and turning, starting the long unhurried journey back out again. Slow waves, spread thin and lacy, shush at your toes. The water is blue-green and sparkly with sunlight. The urge to be in it is almost overwhelming.

You don't say 'ready'. Instead, you step in and say, 'Oh my God. This is wonderful.' And he steps in next to you.

'It's not even cold, is it? It's like a bath,' you say, stepping further in, the water rising to your knees, and above.

You remain a foot or two away from him, near enough to grab if necessary, but not wanting to nanny him. Not wanting him to catch your nervousness.

Out of the corner of your eye you watch. He is concentrating. Wendy is lighter than he is used to, untested in the wide sea, and he is walking carefully with his arms held slightly out, as if on a tightrope. You look away but stay near, alert, listening to the water swirl past him as he steps through it.

The sea is warm but cooler than you and it slides deliciously up your hot skin. When it is at waist height, or just a little higher, you look at him and say, 'Right, I'm going in' and plunge forwards, submerging completely.

Briefly you are in another world, muted and slow. The sea muffles your ears with the sounds of drowning. Your scalp cools and tingles. Your hair stands up, splays out like thistledown.

The sun is hot on your head as soon as you burst up out of the sea again, hair plastered over your face, laughing and gasping, salt at the back of your throat. Pushing your wet hair back, you catch his eye, grinning. It is a challenge. And he grins back at you, and tips forwards, into the water.

Wendy is light and full of air until she has filled with water, and she has not yet filled. She acts like a float. His leg rises suddenly to the surface and forces his head under. The metal in his arm is heavy. His body, this body he has now, is a stranger to the sea, and knows less about it than his mind does. It does not react the way his memory expects. You haven't spoken about it, but you have both known it could be like this, at first. He is struggling.

You fight against the impulse to help him. You don't make a fuss. You stand near and hold back, watching and waiting, hoping you won't need to step in to rescue him and, in doing so, turn the whole escapade into a disaster. He needs to know he can keep himself safe. He thrashes momentarily, then gets his head up again and, as Wendy fills with water, his legs down. He swears and spits, laughing. Then he plunges forwards again, and this time he floats with his head up. He is laughing and spluttering and he is floating in the sea. It is a moment of piercing bliss for you to have shared this landmark. You shout, 'Yeeehaaa!' and plunge underwater again.

The sun has been on the estuary all day, evaporating the sea to something rich and thick. You are buoyed up, floating without effort, under a pink and orange sky. You watch your arms moving through the clear water as you swim. You watch his confidence come swirling back. You are there in the sea for what seems like hours, talking, laughing, basking. Playing and swimming and not swimming, floating on your back, arms and legs pushed out like starfish, the sun still hot on your face. Gulls wheel and cry overhead and you close your eyes, the sunset shining red through your eyelids.

'People fly all the way to the Med to do this,' you say at one point, sculling past him and making little waves that rock him in the water. 'And this is on our doorstep. How lucky are we?' You feel you are the happiest, luckiest woman alive.

Dusk comes. You are standing still, neck deep in the soft warm water, arms around each other. Your cheek is against his shoulder and his is resting on the top of your head as the sky shifts down through purple and umpteen shades of dark blue. Stars appear and a fingernail moon rises. Even the moonlight is hot.

You dress without drying too carefully. You have forgotten to bring underwear. You will go home tonight to drink wine with wrinkled fingers. And you will climb into bed together, your bones feeling cool inside your skin, and kiss the salt off each other.

Ragworm

Pat Sibbons

'Come in, Cassie. Take a seat over there. It really is good to meet you at last.'

Dr Rosemary Ellis closed the door behind her and followed Cassie over to the matching blue sofas.

Cassie wriggled about on the soft fabric until she felt comfortable. She beamed up at Dr Ellis. 'I just love blue. The colour of summer skies and the ocean.'

Dr Ellis sat down opposite her and opened her laptop. 'I have heard so much about you, Cassie. I am really pleased you have come to see me today.'

'Well, Nathaniel said you wanted to talk to me and so I thought, *Why not? Might be fun!*'

'I hope it is going to be fun. Can I get you a drink before we start?'

'A cherry cola would be fantastic,' said Cassie excitedly. 'I just love, love, love cherry cola.'

'No problem. I've messaged my secretary and she will get that for you. Let's begin our chat by getting to know each other. Why don't you start by telling me all about yourself.'

'Well, I'm eleven, going on twelve. My birthday is the 8th of May. My favourite colour is blue, but I guess you already know that. I love Donny Osmond so obviously I hate

David Cassidy. I like dancing, swimming and roller skating.'

'Thank you, Cassie. That's great. And what about friends? Do you have many friends?'

'No. Nathaniel says friends just cause you pain in the long run. Friends all turn out to be snakes. Friends tell and you can't trust blabbermouths.'

'I have spoken to Nathaniel,' said Dr Ellis, 'and he tells me that he has friends. He told me he had a girlfriend when he last came to see me.'

Cassie shrieked with laughter. 'Oh man! He is such a liar, liar pants on fire. He hasn't got a girlfriend. Girls don't like boys like Nathaniel and anyway, Florence wouldn't let him have one.'

'So, are you and Nathaniel close, Cassie?'

'Well, no, not exactly. We don't really like the same things. He is nineteen after all. I suppose I look up to him. If I'm scared I try to find him. Either him or Martha. Martha is lovely. She hugs me when I cry. She whispers little songs in my ear. It makes me feel better.'

'What does Nathaniel look like, Cassie?'

'You know what he looks like, Doctor! You have met him lots of times,' said Cassie looking quizzical.

'Yes, I know how *I* would describe him but I just wanted to know how *you* would describe him.'

'Okay. Well, he is quite tall, he has black skin. He is probably good looking, I suppose. He has a nice smile, when he smiles. He talks quietly so you must listen hard when he talks. He is cool, I think.'

Dr Ellis looked up from her screen. 'Yes, that sounds like

Nathaniel to me. He looks nothing like you, does he, Cassie?'

Cassie roared with laughter. 'Of course not. Why would he?'

Dr Ellis laughed along with her. 'I know. Silly question. Why would he? So, if you were describing to someone how you look, what would you say?'

Cassie thought for a moment. 'Well, I'm quite short for my age. I have pale, blonde hair. I have awful freckles. I'm funny and a bit too loud.'

The doctor smiled at her. 'That's great, Cassie. A good description of yourself. What about Martha? What is she like?'

'Martha is really, really old so her hair is white. She is skinny but her hugs don't feel bony. Her skin is wrinkly but her smile is so sweet.'

There was a knock on the door and the secretary brought in a tray with a cherry cola and a plate of Oreo cookies. She placed the tray on the table between the sofas.

'Wowser!' shouted Cassie. 'Can I have some cookies with my cola, please?'

'Of course. Help yourself.'

Cassie took a large gulp of the fizzy liquid and then shoved a cookie into her mouth.

'I'm really enjoying our chat, Cassie. So, how would you describe Florence?'

Cassie immediately put down her glass and glared at the doctor. 'I'm not talking about her. I hate her. She is mean and horrible. I keep away from her but she is always doing

31

bad stuff to Nathaniel and the others. She is a nasty woman.'

'I'm sorry to have mentioned her, Cassie. Nathaniel told me that she is a large, white woman in her thirties with short, brown hair. Is that correct?'

'She is an ugly, evil, fat bitch. That's what she is. She does look like Nathaniel said, though.'

'I am truly sorry to talk to you about her. Do you think she would talk to me?'

'No, and you wouldn't want to meet her. She just upsets everything. She hurts people. I try to keep away from her. We all do.'

Cassie picked up her glass again, and resumed the massacre of the cookie and cola.

'So, Cassie, I was just wondering. Are you the youngest? I think I remember Lorali telling me that there was a little girl with you all.'

'Well, Lorali is a blabbermouth. No one is meant to know about Connie. Connie is only tiny. We agreed to keep her out of all this. Lorali just can't keep her big mouth shut! I suppose Lorali sat on this sofa, sipping tea, telling you all sorts of secret stuff. I like Lorali but I wish she would keep quiet.'

Cassie placed her empty glass on the tray and angrily wiped her mouth with the back of her hand.

'I won't ask you about Connie then as I see it upsets you.'

'I'm not upset. I'm just fed up with Lorali thinking she is the big I am! She is only two years older than me but she thinks she is so much cleverer and more grown up. She isn't.

Do you know she wets the bed all the time? And she can't tie her shoe laces! I know all kinds of stuff about her but I'm not telling. I'm not a super bitch.'

Dr Ellis put her laptop down on the sofa next to her. 'I think that's very grown up of you, Cassie. I bet you look out for Connie all the time as she is so little?'

'I do. I have to. She is only two and so I have to look after her. She can't even talk properly yet. I love her chubby little arms around my neck when I cuddle her and kiss her. Her hair smells of baby shampoo. She can't say "Cassie" so, obviously, she can't say "Nathaniel".' Cassie hesitated before continuing. 'She just says, "Momma".'

Tears began to roll down Cassie's cheeks and she flicked them away, the broad grin returning to her lips.

'Well, Cassie, it has been wonderful meeting you. Do you think you would like to come again for a chat another time?'

'Maybe,' said Cassie, getting up. 'If there are more cookies and cherry cola I will probably come back. I'll talk to Nathaniel about it.'

Dr Ellis walked over to the door and opened it.

'Goodbye, Cassie.'

'See ya later alligator,' said the woman in the smart business suit, with grey flecked auburn hair, as she passed through the waiting room and out into the street beyond.

L'Esprit de Collette

Barbara Sleap

Mark and I stood looking at the ramshackle exterior of 'Le Petit Coin'. We could see past the broken gate, the overgrown frontage and the smeared windows; it was just what we had been searching for over the last few months since we had decided on a French Getaway.

Mark turned the heavy, old key in the lock and, opening the top half of the stable door, reached inside to pull up the latch. The door opened with a creak and we stepped over the threshold into the dark interior. As we stood in the doorway, a cold shiver engulfed me. Mark, however, was already busy enthusing about the huge old fireplace.

'Wow, look at that. Imagine cosy nights in front of a real fire, Jules. We could really make something of this place. Let's explore.'

We entered the kitchen, completely bare except for an old stained and chipped porcelain sink. There was a large door in the corner and I tentatively opened it to reveal bare shelves. On hearing scurrying, I shut the door quickly.

'It's only a larder,' I said, but I felt an uncomfortable shiver again. I wanted to leave as soon as possible.

'There are three bedrooms, Jules, and it's bigger than all the others we've seen. Come on, what's up? You seem quiet.

Don't you think it's just perfect?'

'There just seems to be a mountain of work to be done, Mark. When would we get the time?'

'But, Jules, it's in a great location, near to Vilaine. It's the right price and the right size. Come on.'

With that he bounded up the rickety stairway. I followed meekly. We inspected the bedrooms, all bare apart from the largest which contained a threadbare piece of carpet but did have a lovely view over the fields leading to the river. There was what had once been a bathroom with another stained sink in the corner. The toilet was filthy.

'Soon get a shower and new toilet in here, could be done in a couple of days.' Mark was beaming.

Still, I couldn't get rid of the horrible shivery feeling; it felt as though someone was following me, although I wouldn't have been able to explain it. Mark continued to gabble on about kitchen units, showers and flooring. All I wanted was to get some air.

'I'm going to look outside,' I said.

The garden was a jungle apart from a small patch at one side that was remarkably tidy and had geraniums and begonias in full flower. This seemed weird as the rest of the area was completely overgrown.

I went back inside to find Mark and suggested we return to the hotel for lunch.

'I don't think we need to see any more, do we?' he said. 'This is just what we want.'

We had more viewings arranged for the next day but, after lunch, Mark wanted to go back to the house to make notes and take photos. I had other ideas. I wanted to look around the small town of Villaines-la-Juhel. I said I would drop him off and pick him up later.

Collette heard the door shut... It was that man again. Didn't he know he wasn't wanted here, with his big ideas of changing her cottage into some sort of holiday home? The girl wasn't with him this time. Collette knew she could feel her presence; she could sense her discomfort. Collette had managed to keep many people away over the years; most of them had left quickly. But this man seemed immune. Perhaps she was losing her touch.

Mark entered the cottage; it felt colder somehow. Undeterred, he walked around making notes. He photographed the bathroom and took a few measurements. *This would have to be the first job,* he thought. His friend Colin was a plumber; they could come over for a long weekend, stay at the hotel and get a few things done. He pulled his jacket closely round him. God it was cold in here, he hadn't noticed it that morning. Anyway, it would certainly be warm when they got a wood fire burning. He imagined sitting cosily in its glow sharing a bottle of red wine and toasting their good fortune.

He was inspecting the old staircase when he noticed an indentation under the stairway. He soon realised it was a door. There wasn't a handle but using his trusty penknife he managed to slide it into the small gap. The door opened and he used the small torch he had brought with him to reveal a narrow wooden stairway. *It must be a cellar*, he thought. He gingerly stepped onto the top step; it felt steady so he moved to the next one. Shining the light around, he saw a large empty space with a few bits of dilapidated furniture piled in the corner. As he began to descend further, Mark sensed something behind him. As he turned to look, he felt a vague push. He lost his footing and fell blindly headfirst into the gloom and onto the concrete floor below. Blackness consumed him.

***

After a pleasant stroll around the varied little shops and a peep in the old church I stopped for a coffee at the patisserie, unable to resist one of their sumptuous cakes to accompany it. I spoke to the elderly owner of the patisserie and asked her about Le Petit Coin. I was shaken when she told me the cottage had been empty for ten years since the current owner's grandmother, Collette, had died. Eugene Patrice owned the cottage but lived in Spain and had let it deteriorate. There had been a family feud since the old lady's husband was killed during World War I. Eugene's mother had married a local farmer against the old lady's wishes leaving Collette alone to become a virtual recluse. Some said the cottage was haunted and there were also reports of a mysterious flowerbed which still bloomed in the untended garden.

I drove back to the old cottage expecting to see the door open, but it was locked. I tried to walk round the side but there were large bramble bushes blocking an old wooden gate. I banged on the door and called Mark's name but an eerie silence ensued. I tried ringing Mark's mobile but it seemed to be switched off. Feeling uneasy, I drove to the hotel. Mark must have finished and made his way back. I needed to tell him the story of Le Petit Coin, then perhaps he wouldn't be so keen. At the hotel, I asked the owner if Mark had returned and he shook his head.

'Non, Mark, he has not returned.' He turned to point to the hook behind him. 'The key is still missing but it is okay, I have another one.'

He handed me the key and I rushed up to room 10. It was just as we had left it at lunchtime. I drove frantically to the immobiliere, Tomas, and explained the dilemma. He seemed very concerned and said he would drive me to Le Petit Coin with a spare key.

On arrival, Tomas opened the door and we entered the dim interior. It seemed colder than ever. I called out for Mark but there was just silence. Then I saw his notebook, pen and mobile lying on the floor. Hoping for a clue I picked up the notebook but there were only a few measurements written there. His mobile showed my message and a few pictures of the old bathroom. We both noticed the small door, which was slightly open, at the same time. Tomas peered in using his phone torch and made his way down the steps. After some minutes he called me and I descended the stairway apprehensively.

'Mark,' I called out, rushing over to his prone body. He was unconscious and lying in a crooked position on the concrete floor.

Tomas was kneeling by Mark's side, holding his wrist. 'I

can feel a pulse,' he said, before bounding up the stairs to call the emergency services, leaving me alone in the darkness with Mark.

***

It was six weeks before we arrived back in England. Luckily, Mark was expected to make a full recovery. He had suffered severe concussion, a broken hip, arm and ankle. After he told me what had happened, and that he was certain he had been pushed rather than fallen, we soon shelved the idea of a French retreat. We decided, instead, to buy a modern apartment on the sunny Costa del Sol.

Collette watched as the middle-aged couple inspected her cottage. She knew the woman could sense her presence as she began nudging her husband towards the front door.

'I don't like it, Ted, it gives me the creeps, let's go. There's something not right here, hurry up we've others to see.' With that they made a hasty retreat.

Collette smiled to herself, glad to be alone again. No one would have this cottage. It was hers and always would be.

Dotty Nonsense

Trisha Todd

Jenni had been busy. She had noted the many news reports of an exceedingly contagious virus spreading across the world and had prepared, using money she had squirrelled away from the housekeeping, and a bonus payment from her employer. In the week since the government had announced everyone was to stay indoors, she had painted her spare room a pale whisper grey and installed oak laminate flooring. She had plucked up courage to use her husband's electric drill, and had managed to fix up shelving, even getting them level, which was more than her accident-prone husband could do.

She had bought a white desk to fit under the wide window, which looked over her compact back garden, and she now sat in her new, black, faux leather chair and opened her top drawer with excitement. There, arranged in rows of colour, were bottles of craft paint, some matt, some metallic, some for inside or outside use, but all full of promise. The pencil pot on the desktop contained acrylic rods of various sizes, together with round-ended rods she had seen nail artists use, on the rare occasions she had a manicure.

Jenni looked at the large, round stone she had placed on the silicon mat in front of her, then at the paint bottles. Which colours should she choose? She had already painted the stone in black acrylic, and stencilled on the guidelines, and wanted something to really 'pop'. Out came the white bottle, followed by the turquoise and then an iridescent purple. She set them out in front of her, almost reverently, and then squeezed a small amount of each into her plastic paint tray.

She took an acrylic rod and dipped the end into the white paint, making sure it was properly coated. Her hand hovered over the centre point of the stone, shaking. Taking a deep breath to steady herself, she carefully placed a dot in the centre of her pattern. The dot was perfect, round and domed and dead centre. Jenni smiled and sighed in relief as she wiped the paint off the rod.

Next, she took a rounded nail rod and, just as carefully, placed smaller dots around the larger one, making sure they were all the same size, and equally spaced. She continued placing dots, changing sizes and colours as she went. When dry, she added smaller dots on top, to highlight certain areas, the circles and swoops covering the stone in a mesmerising mix of colour and pattern. She sat back and admired her work; her first mandala stone was finished. She glanced at the wall clock and was surprised to see that it was mid-afternoon and the sandwich she had made for lunch sat forgotten on a plate.

***

The following day, Jenni was again in her craft room, dotting a plain wooden jewellery box, and the day after that, she dotted a photo frame. She ordered some silicon moulds and plaster of Paris, and made some tea light holders, hearts, and trinket jars, and dotted them. She took her husband's beer and wine bottles out of the recycling and dotted them too. She ordered fabric paint and dotted her T-shirts. She was obsessed with dots.

Malcolm, her husband, was quite happy for Jenni to disappear into her room, day after day, and joked he was a dotting widower. It gave him free rein of the television remote control, and he spent a lot of his time lounging on the sofa, watching re-runs of war films and westerns. He wasn't remotely interested in going out for an hour's permitted exercise, and wasn't too bothered that the waistband on his trousers was getting steadily tighter as the lockdown weeks passed, after all, who was going to notice?

Jenni dotted everything she could lay her hands on, until there was nothing left, and decided to take one last look around the house in case she had missed something. Seeing Malcolm asleep on the sofa, she looked at his bald patch. She couldn't, could she?

Breaking Bread

Kim Kimber

Marsha loved bread. Everything about it. From the distinct, yeasty smell and slightly salty taste to the springy texture and the way a freshly baked loaf would break apart in her fingers. Not the unappetising processed bread you can buy in the supermarket but the kind of miracle created in her kitchen from a few simple ingredients. Over the years she had made every kind of bread from doughy farmhouse loaves to dense, olive focaccia, but her favourite was traditional home-baked coco bread, made with coconut milk, using her Jamaican mother's recipe. A family favourite, it reminded her of happier times when the children were at home and she still had a purpose.

For Marsha, the days during lockdown were long. Each one stretched out before her full of possibility, hours to be filled with productivity and purpose. But she did not spend her time in any useful way. It was a good day if she managed to get out of bed and take a shower.

Her four children checked in with her from time to time.

'Hi Mama, how ya doin'?'

Marsha would give her usual response. '*Mi deh yah, yuh know*, don't worry about me.' And so they didn't. The children's father had left them before Shadea, the youngest, had been born. In the years that followed, Marsha's life had revolved around the children and she had filled their home with so much love, they hardly noticed the missing parent.

As her family grew up, Marsha had few rules but insisted they sat round the table together every night for dinner. Then they would share stories about their day, as they passed round a basket of bread to accompany their meal; 'breaking bread' she believed it was called. She had looked the expression up on Google and discovered it originated in the Bible with Jesus and his Disciples. Anyway, it seemed exactly right in Marsha's house where there was always freshly baked bread on the table at family mealtimes.

When the children left home, two for university and careers in medicine and education, one to work as a fashion designer in Paris, and Shadea to move in with her boyfriend Tom, Marsha was lonely. She loved holidays and celebrations when they could come together to share a meal, providing her with an excuse to bake. During lockdown, Marsha had formed a 'bubble' with Shadea and Tom but their visits mostly comprised of her keeping an eye on their boisterous new puppy, Lucky, that Shadea had bought to ease the long days of furlough and curbed freedom. Unsupervised, Lucky would chew his way through anything in his path; clothes, furniture and shoes. Marsha was always secretly relieved when they took him home.

One evening, as Marsha sat eating supper (baked beans on sliced, shop bought bread, something she would have sneered at before the pandemic), a news report caught her attention. Usually, Marsha avoided the news as it was full of sad statistics, and medical experts and disagreeable politicians arguing, but she was flicking through the channels to find something to watch before the start of *EastEnders*. The lead story made her pause. According to the newsreader, bread had suddenly become unavailable due to a national shortage of flour. The report was accompanied by images of empty shelves and bewildered shoppers with trolleys full of toilet rolls, but no bread.

Putting down her plate, Marsha padded into the kitchen. She opened drawers and cupboards, pulling out utensils, two jars of dried yeast, tins of coconut milk and, to her joy, several bags of unopened flour. There was strong flour, whole-wheat flour, rye flour; each perfect for making different types of bread. Some of the flour was slightly out of date, but not by much. Her TV dinner and favourite soap forgotten, Marsha put on her apron and did what she loved to do most; bake bread. The kitchen was soon obscured by a flour mist as she worked, her body relaxing into the familiar, calming rhythm of mixing and kneading. She waited for the dough to rise, before kneading again and fashioning the stretchy, elastic bread mixture into oblongs, squares and small round buns. Marsha had rejected Shadea's offer to buy her a bread maker. To her mind, it was not proper bread-making unless your arms ached and your knuckles were sore from all that kneading. A few hours later, every surface was full of loaves and baps of different shapes and sizes and the familiar, comforting aroma of freshly baked bread once more filled the kitchen.

The next morning Marsha didn't linger in bed as usual

but instead rose early. The smell of last night's baking still hung in the air and pulled her to the kitchen where the result of her labour lay in batches covering the work surfaces. She cut herself a generous slice from a farmhouse loaf, topped it with butter and let out a satisfied sigh at the slight crunch as she bit into the crust.

When her appetite had been sated, she switched on the kettle and sat down at her kitchen table to think. There was a bread shortage; she had more than enough and the means to make more. She might not be able to solve the nation's problems but she could certainly provide for her neighbours. The only question was how to get it to them; there was a lockdown, after all. Marsha's shopping was now delivered weekly by a cheery deliveryman, and she rarely left the house these days.

Marsha lived in a two-bedroomed bungalow, with a small lounge and spacious kitchen, the latter being the only reason she had allowed her children to persuade her to move from the family home. The bungalow was one amongst several others of uniform shape and size, largely populated by elderly couples and women on their own, like herself. Marsha was on nodding terms with most of them and had graduated to a friendly 'good morning' with one or two. Unfortunately, she had moved in three months before the government put a stop to any kind of socialising, curbing the opportunity to form meaningful friendships.

Marsha knew she couldn't expect people to answer their doors to a near stranger in the middle of a pandemic so she opened the laptop Shadea had given her enabling her to take part in zoom calls (how wonderful to see her family on the screen) and typed up a simple note: 'Free home-baked bread delivered to your door. Message me to show your interest, Marsha, no. 93'. She added her mobile number and printed out several copies. She then put on her coat, hat, gloves and mask and stepped outside for the first time in weeks. Less than an hour later, Marsha had delivered leaflets to every house in her road. She went indoors, made a cup of tea and sat down to wait.

She had barely taken a sip from her mug when the messages started coming in. 'Yes, please' from Ida at no. 91; 'How lovely, thank you' from Bob at 29 and 'We are desperate for bread, so count us in' from Pam and George, who reside at no. 54. For the remainder of the morning, Marsha's phoned pinged with messages. After a brief lunch, she carefully wrapped each loaf and batch of coco bread in plastic wrapping, packed her shopping trolley and went outside.

It took Marsha a couple of hours to make her deliveries. At each house she would ring the bell or knock loudly, place her gift on the doorstep and step well back. She was met with cheery waves and smiling faces, or as far as she could tell behind the various masks. Several people offered to pay her but she refused every time. Returning home, Marsha felt energised and full of purpose. She felt useful again.

News spread fast and Marsha received more messages and orders. But she didn't have enough ingredients to bake, so she politely declined, explaining the reason. Then, it was Marsha's turn to be surprised as her neighbours dug around in the back of their cupboards and donated half-opened bags of long-forgotten flour of all varieties, delivered to her doorstep.

She was delighted that her traditional coco bread was very popular and frequently requested. It didn't take long for the local press to learn about the amazing woman who was supplying the community with bread made from leftover bits of flour and Marsha became somewhat of a celebrity in her home town. The neighbourhood food bank contacted her to ask if she could bake some bread for them to help feed local families. They had supplies of flour and yeast, if she was interested. Marsha said she was.

A short time later, she registered her little business with the council and booked an online course in food hygiene which she hoped wouldn't be beyond her limited computer skills.

And Marsha continued baking. She made batches of loaves which were picked up by volunteers, delivered to the food bank and distributed to the needy. She hadn't been so busy in a very long time.

Lockdown ended two weeks after the successful completion of her course, along with the flour shortage, the same day Marsha found herself trending on something called Twitter. Suddenly, everyone wanted to know her. What was her secret? Could she share her recipe for coco bread? Had she considered a recipe book? Would she like to appear on daytime TV with Phil and Holly?

Shortly afterwards, Shadea phoned.

'Hey, Mama, I was wondering if you could look after

Lucky for a couple of hours in the morning. Tom's back at work and I have to pop into the office.'

'I'd love to…' replied Marsha.

'Good, I knew we could reply on you, only no one else is able to have–'

'…any other time, but I'm afraid I can't tomorrow.'

There was a slightly surprised harrumph on the other end of the phone as her daughter waited to find out what could be more important than her and her mischievous puppy.

'I'm going to be on *This Morning*, teaching the nation how to bake coco bread.'

White Feathers

Lois Maulkin

'Isn't this all a bit silly?' I asked.

'Silly yourself,' said my next door but three neighbour, Jenny, peering into the depths of my teacup. Jenny turned the cup this way and that in her hands, holding it to the light, putting her reading glasses on, taking them off, pursing her lips and saying 'oooh' and 'aaaah', and 'yes, that makes sense', as she gazed into its depths. I rolled my eyes.

'You're rolling your eyes,' said Jenny, still looking into the cup.

'Is that what the tea leaves are telling you?'

'No, that's what being your best friend for forty years is telling me,' said Jenny. 'You always roll your eyes when I'm trying to help you in an esoteric fashion.'

'Can you wonder?' I said, yawning and looking at the clock on Jenny's kitchen wall. 'I'll have to go in a moment, Jen. Someone's coming to look at the house at three and I need to tidy the kitchen.'

'Right,' said Jenny, putting the cup on its saucer and her elbows on the table. She looked at me over the top of her glasses. 'The tea leaves tell me you have had worries recently but there is a new home and happiness ahead. And white feathers will be coming to guide you.'

'Is that it?' I said, laughing and putting on my coat. 'We've been talking about my house move for months now. It's hardly a revelation, is it? Thanks for the tea, Jenny, and thanks for trying to cheer me up.'

I left her house by the front door, trotted a couple of houses along and let myself into mine. She is a good friend, Jenny, *but she does talk a lot of hot air sometimes,* I thought as I put my old, padded coat away in the cupboard under the stairs.

I washed up my lunch things, swiped a mop across the floor and had just wiped down the kitchen surfaces when there was a ring at the doorbell. As I approached the front door I noticed a feather on the doormat. It was an inch or so long, very white and clean looking. I picked it up, put it in my pocket and opened the door.

Mr and Mrs Greenleaf were a pleasant young couple who obviously liked the house as I showed them round.

'We're hoping to start a family,' smiled Mrs Greenleaf, staring into the living room as they made their way to the front door. 'We've looked at dozens of places, waiting to find one that feels like home, like this one.' As they stepped outside I felt the beginnings of hope tingling through me.

The estate agent phoned me an hour later to say that Mr and Mrs Greenleaf had made an offer of the full asking price for my house. Delighted, I pulled on my coat and hurried up the road to tell Jenny.

'I told you better times were coming,' she said, putting the kettle on. 'It was all there, plain as day, in your cup.'

'There was tea in my cup but I think any messages came

from your imagination,' I said, smiling and passing Jenny two clean cups from the draining board.

'What's this?' Jenny put her finger into one of the cups and pulled out a small white feather. I remembered the feather from my doormat and pulled it out of my jeans pocket to show Jenny. Laughing, I told her how I'd found it just before I'd let in Mr and Mrs Greenleaf.

'There you are!' Jenny was triumphant. 'The tea leaves were right when they said white feathers would come to guide you. Angels send them, you know.'

'Don't be ridiculous.' I reached for her biscuit tin. 'It's pure coincidence. Mind if I take this last Garibaldi?'

The following day I started flat hunting in earnest. I had lived happily in my house for many years, but my pension was not all I had hoped it would be and, unless I wanted to live on gruel and ration my heating, the sensible thing was to move into a smaller place and free up some capital. I hoped I wouldn't have to move too far from Jenny, who had been my best friend for almost as long as we had lived in the same road.

Now my house had a 'Sold' sign going up outside, I felt free to look around local flats. I made an appointment to meet the estate agent at 72 Sunshine Gardens, which was a few minutes' drive away, at 10 o'clock in the morning. I parked my car at the kerb. The estate agent was smiling on the doorstep and we went in together. The flat was large and airy with wintery light streaming in through big windows. There were views over the park.

'This is lovely,' I said to the estate agent as we walked

round the empty rooms. I stood at the kitchen sink and looked out of the window, briefly watching a middle-aged couple in matching anoraks throwing a Frisbee for a spaniel, and turned to say to the estate agent that I didn't think I'd need to see any other properties. There, in the middle of the empty kitchen floor, was a small white feather. Suddenly uneasy, I changed my mind. As we left, I arranged to meet the estate agent the next day at another flat.

'See you at eleven-thirty,' I said, opening the car door. There on the seat was a small white feather. The hair on the back of my neck prickled and I got in and drove straight to Jenny's.

'What's going on?' I asked. 'I keep finding feathers.'

'I told you,' said Jenny, 'angels send them. It's nothing to worry about, it's a good sign. Honestly it is. Shall I read your tarot before lunch?'

'No, thank you,' I said crisply.

The following day was warmer and sunnier. The fine weather cheered me and I felt full of hope as I pulled on my denim jacket to go to my next flat viewing. I kept looking for white feathers to appear and was pleased that none did. I saw three more flats that day but, nice though they were, they couldn't match the flat at Sunshine Gardens. I arranged with the estate agent to have a second viewing of number 72 the following afternoon.

I dreamed that night I was standing in the flat at Sunshine Gardens, with yellow light flooding in through all the windows and feathers coming down, thick and fast, like a blizzard, settling into a white carpet that reached higher than my knees. I woke up in a panic. There seemed something sinister about the feathers. I'm not a great one for magic and mystery. I know things happen that science cannot explain and we cannot understand and, personally speaking, I think we're not meant to understand them and they should be left well alone. I felt the white feathers, rather than encouraging me to buy the flat at Sunshine Gardens, were the one thing that put me off.

I went to see Jenny after breakfast, demanding she tell me all about the white feathers. 'What do you want to know? There's marmalade in the cupboard.' She slid a piece of buttered toast onto a plate and pushed it across the table towards me.

'Are they evil? And is it lime?'

'No and no, angelic and orange,' said Jenny sitting down opposite me.

'Look,' she stirred her coffee, 'it's just feathers. People say that angels send them as a message that all is well. It's nothing to worry about; it's actually a very positive sign.'

'Well, it doesn't feel very positive,' I said, opening a jar of Jenny's homemade Seville Thick Shred, 'it feels malevolent.'

'Malevolent? I made it fresh last week,' said Jenny, deliberately misunderstanding.

After my second breakfast of the morning, I put on my coat and set off to Sunshine Gardens for my second viewing of the flat.

The estate agent said, 'I'll wait by the front door and let you have a look round on your own.' Smiling broadly, I wandered from room to room, imagining my sofa here, my coffee table there, my pictures on the walls.

'I really feel this is the place for me,' I said, crossing the small hall to go into the bedroom again.

'It's very nice, isn't it?' said the estate agent. 'Have you noticed this built-in cupboard?' I turned to look at the cupboard and saw a white feather float down past her purple skirt and land on her foot. The back of my neck prickled.

'You've, er, you've got a feather on your shoe,' I said, my voice coming out high and uncertain.

'Oh, yes.' She picked it up and put it in her jacket pocket. 'Isn't that supposed to be lucky?'

'I'm not sure,' I said, entering the bedroom again. There were three white feathers scattered across the grey carpet. I hurried out through the hall into the living room. Several white feathers on the windowsill in here and two on the floor just inside the door. And none of them had been there when I looked moments before. Panic rose in me and I rushed into the kitchen. Two white feathers by the sink, one in the sink, three by the stove. Suddenly, it was all too much. 'I'm sorry,' I said, 'I'll have to think about it,' making a run for the front door. There was a white feather on the doormat and a couple blowing about along the path.

I got into my car – another feather on the dashboard – and drove straight to Jenny's.

'You'll have to make them stop,' I said, marching into her house as she opened the door.

'Make what stop?' she hurried up the hall behind me. 'What on earth's the matter?'

'All these feathers,' I said miserably. 'I really like the flat at Sunshine Gardens. It's lovely, the rooms are a great size, it's airy and has a nice, comfortable feeling. It overlooks the park. It's near enough for us to see each other most days. It's almost perfect. But I feel there's something peculiar about it, something spooky, because everywhere I look there are all these white feathers you say are from the angels.' I put my head in my hands. 'I feel like crying, Jen. It's the only thing wrong with it. It's like they're following me. Everywhere I turn today there are white feathers. It's frightening me.' I realised I sounded at best verging on hysterical and at worst completely unhinged.

I pulled out my usual chair to sit at her kitchen table and a dozen or so small white feathers flurried out across the floor. 'Look!' I squeaked, pointing. 'They're everywhere!'

'Oh my goodness,' Jenny came round the table to look, 'so they are. What's going on?' She paused for a moment, looked me up and down and started laughing.

'You can go off people, you know,' I said, at a loss. 'It's not funny.'

Jenny chuckled a bit more and said, 'Oh, but it is. They're coming from you.'

I looked at her silently for a moment. 'Are you saying I'm an angel?'

'Of course not,' said Jenny, making no attempt to hold back her mirth. 'You've torn your coat, that's all. All the feathers from inside are coming out.'

I pulled off my coat and held it out and saw that, just under one sleeve, there was an inch-long tear. And several little white feathers were making their way out. Relief overwhelmed me and I caught Jenny's eye and we both gave in to laughter. No wonder I'd been finding little white feathers all over the place; I'd been shedding them myself. Happily, I took my phone from my pocket.

'I'm going to put in an offer on the flat at Sunshine Gardens,' I said, 'now I know it's not haunted.'

'Shall I read your leaves for you before you call?' said Jenny, reaching for the pot.

'No thank you,' I said happily. 'All I want from your teapot is a nice strong cup of tea.'

Flip Side

Barbara Sleap

Zoe took complete charge of the batter and carefully followed Marie's instructions, but Liam insisted on cracking the eggs into the flour and having a turn with the electric whisk. After much bickering and a work surface covered in flour and milk, the batter was finally made.

'Sorry, Mum. We've made a bit of a mess. Don't worry, I'll clean it up.'

Marie smiled. Her daughter was always helpful. Liam, however, was a typical ten-year-old boy and immediately disappeared into his bedroom to play.

A while later, they heard Tom's key in the lock.

'Hi guys. I'm home,' he called out.

As usual, he gave each member of his family an affectionate hug, and patted Marie's dog, Sheba. Before he could say anything else, Zoe said, 'Dad, can we make pancakes now, please? We've been waiting ages. Mum refused to start frying them until you came home.'

'And quite right too. I wouldn't want to miss out on all the fun.'

On hearing his dad's voice, Liam came running down the stairs. A friendly argument ensued about who should fry and toss the first pancake. Zoe insisted it should be her as she had contributed most to making the batter. Liam said it should be him as he was the oldest, albeit only by half an hour! Tom took out a coin from his pocket and Marie called 'heads for Zoe' and 'tails for Liam'. Tails won. Zoe stuck her tongue out at Liam as he gave her a gloating grin.

'Mum, he's making faces, tell him off.'

'She stuck her tongue out first.'

The twins quickly forgot about being cross with one another as their dad poured oil into a frying pan. Liam's first effort was a scrunched up mess but he tipped it on a plate, covered it with jam and sugar and ate it greedily. Zoe's pancake landed half in, half out of the pan and, to Liam's annoyance, she was given another try which was only slightly better than the first.

There was enough batter to make three pancakes each with some left over for Marie and Tom. Tom confidently flipped his over and was able to slide a perfect pancake onto his plate. The twins clapped and Sheba barked. Tom gave a little bow.

'It's Mum's turn now,' shouted the children in unison.

Marie shook her head. 'No, I can't do it, you know that. It'll just end up on the floor. You can have another go and make mine for me.'

Tom grabbed her hand. 'Come on, love. Let's give it a try.'

He added a bit more oil to the pan and poured in a small amount of batter. He let the pancake cook for a minute and then placed the pan in Marie's outstretched hands.

'Right, now flip.'

With a quick jerk of her hands, Marie flipped the pancake over. It landed rather unevenly back in the pan.

'Look at that, kids. Mum's been practising,' Tom said. The twins cheered in encouragement.

'I knew you could do it, Marie,' he said in her ear. 'You're always so capable. Just because you are blind doesn't mean you can't toss a pancake.'

The children giggled. Marie smiled as Sheba quietly came up to her mistress, tail wagging, and gave her hand a lick of approval.

Meeting Patrick

Sue Duggans

I first met Patrick and his delightful wife, Sara, back in the summer of 1990. I was staying at my cousin Emily's cottage in the Lake District while she was working away in Brussels. My sole companion was my red setter, Rossi, who lifted my spirits daily. The need for solitude and time to rebuild had brought me to this charming, picturesque, remote location. The recent, unexpected break up with my partner of eight years, the beautiful and talented yet arrogant and eccentric actor Greg Coln, had left me devastated and I required time to recover.

It was a bright but windy day when I walked with Rossi down to the village shop. Striding out with the wind on my cheeks and through my hair, I felt better than I had for some time. It would be difficult to not feel refreshed and strengthened in this wonderful place and I thought about the many poets and artists who had been inspired by the location. When I got to the charming little shop, I tied Rossi to a post outside although I imagine taking him in wouldn't have raised an eyebrow. I was looking at the small selection of teabags stacked neatly on the top shelf when the shopkeeper, Molly, engaged me in conversation. Patrick was standing on the opposite side of the tiny shop with his elbow resting comfortably on the counter. He was dressed smartly with his wavy hair in place, despite the windy weather. I noticed that he was wearing stout walking boots which were polished and immaculate. He was, of course, instantly recognisable. He saw me looking at his boots and with a twinkle in his eye said, 'I don't wear these when I'm dancing,' and did a little twirl. We laughed!

The three of us began conversing comfortably and I found myself divulging more about my private life than I would normally. Molly and Patrick's kindness and warm hand of friendship were greatly appreciated. We chattered for a good fifteen minutes until Rossi's whimpering reminded me that I'd left him outside. I paid for the teabags and before I left Patrick invited me to drop in for a cup of tea with him and his wife the next afternoon. I accepted without hesitation. What a thrill to spend time in the home of such a celebrated individual!

So that's how it started. Several informal get-togethers followed and, by the time I was ready to return to the hubbub of life on the outskirts of London, I felt I could count Patrick and Sara as my friends.

One evening early in December I received a call from Sara. Patrick was travelling to London the following Monday for a publicity shoot to launch his new series and wondered if he could call in on me. My cheeks flushed slightly pink at the thought of him arriving on my doorstep.

'Of course, it will be a pleasure. He must come for supper,' I heard myself saying, while wondering at the same time what I'd cook for her famous and much-loved husband.

We arranged for him to come round at seven the following Tuesday evening which would give me four days to plan, and worry about, our meal together and get the house in order.

As the grandfather clock in the hall was striking seven, the doorbell rang. I shut Rossi in the kitchen and opened the door. Patrick stood there, uncomfortably clutching an imposing bunch of flowers wrapped in silver tissue and tied with ribbon. His cheeks were rosy from the nippy December air.

I greeted him cheerily. 'Hello, Pat,' (Pat being his preferred name). 'How lovely to see you again. Do come in.' He smiled, handed me the flowers and stepped inside. I bent down to kiss his cheek but the sausage-like projection which is his nose nearly poked my eye out!

'Ay up! When they created me, I didn't pick my nose,' he quipped.

As he walked in front of me down the hall, I noticed that he swayed slightly from side to side suggestive of a sailor's, and not a postman's, gait.

I steered him towards the kitchen door and said, 'Straight ahead, Pat.'

When he opened the door, Rossi, who loved to greet visitors, bounded towards Pat and nearly knocked him off his feet. Had it not been for his sturdy Royal Mail-issue boots I think he'd have gone over. I apologised profusely and ordered Rossi to his bed. He looked at me dolefully and complied.

'Do sit down, Pat.' I'd set two places at the small dining

table but manoeuvred Pat towards the taller of the two chairs on which I'd placed a thick cushion. It was a bit of a climb for him to get up but he got there and, thanks to the extra height which the cushion provided, could see over the tabletop. His short legs swung some distance from the floor.

I didn't waste time in getting the hot food on the table. I'd chosen cottage pie with peas and finely-chopped cabbage guessing that it would be easy to manoeuvre into such a tiny, flattened mouth. Luckily, I'd managed to find some discreet children's cutlery, including a very small spoon, in a local shop. Pat ate with enthusiasm then wiped his little mouth with a napkin.

'By 'eck, that was good,' he said, patting his stomach.

I'd made apple crumble with custard for pudding and that was met with the same fervour.

When we had finished our meal, we went into the lounge, which was warm and cosy, to drink our tea. I was keen to learn more about Greendale, the little village in the Lake District where Pat and Sara lived with their son, Julian. I'd become acquainted with a number of local characters during my ten week stay in the summer and held dear this quaint little community and its quirky residents.

Pat spoke passionately about his work as a postman and how it gives him the chance to see his friends and neighbours every day. He paused frequently and ran his hand over his chestnut hair. In a curiously unique way, Pat was attractive despite his out-of-proportion nose, lack of chin and flat face. His eyes twinkled as he spoke and his tiny mouth frequently broke into a cheery smile.

He went on to tell me how important it is for him to have Jess, his little black and white cat, at his side. 'I sometimes think that he's the brains of the outfit,' he said with a characteristic sideways smile.

'And how's Miss Hubbard doing?' I enquired. I'd met her once when I was visiting Pat and Sara. Her 'sit-up-and-beg' bicycle, complete with pannier, was leaning against the garden fence when I arrived. She was a very old-fashioned individual dressed in tweed. Despite her irritatingly high-pitched voice she appeared to be the embodiment of sweetness. For the first time that evening the smile was replaced with a frown. 'My, my, my!' Pat exclaimed. 'Poor Miss Hubbard!'

'Tell me more,' I probed, fascinated.

'Well, back in October when the nights were drawing in, she was off to choir practice on her bicycle. Just on the bend between her cottage and Greendale church she skidded on a patch of oil. She went flying across the road and landed heavily in the ditch.'

'Poor soul!' I exclaimed, although I could feel an uncharitable smile brewing as I imagined the scene: Miss Hubbard, legs in air and bloomers exposed, crying out for *anyone* to help her.

'It was a miracle that Peter Fogg was passing by on his tractor, heading for home after a long day at Greendale Farm.'

'Thank heavens for Peter,' I said. 'So what happened then?'

'Well!' As he spoke, Pat drummed his three little fingers

on the arm of the chair and chuckled a little. 'Pete tried to recover her from the ditch and as soon as he went near her she started screaming blue murder.' At this point Pat lowered his voice. 'Word is that she's never been touched by a man let alone *a farmhand.*'

'And then what?' I asked.

Pat continued, 'The screaming went on and on until the Reverend Timms heard the commotion and ran from the church as fast as he could. Close on his heels came Julia Pottage followed by Mrs Goggins who were already at choir practice. Julia climbed into the ditch and tried to make Miss Hubbard comfortable, wiping her tears with a flowery hanky, and all the while Miss Hubbard sobbed and sobbed. Mrs Goggins hobbled over to Granny Dryden's cottage where she phoned for an ambulance stressing that there *must* be at least one female on board. Miss Hubbard was patched up at the hospital and sent home the next day.'

As Pat described the incident I imagined it had been the talk of the village for days, if not weeks. It was some time before Miss Hubbard got on her bicycle again, Pat went on to say, but she was often seen walking round the village taking every opportunity to talk about her 'unfortunate accident'.

Sam Waldron was overheard telling Alf Thompson that he had an oil leak in his little blue delivery van so, in Miss Hubbard's eyes, he became the main suspect for causing the accident. Thankfully for Sam nothing could be proved.

'More tea, Pat?' I asked.

'Lovely!' he replied, running his tiny pink tongue over his lips.

I got up and went to the kitchen. As I stood waiting for the kettle to boil, I had to pinch myself. 'Is this bizarre experience real? Am I dreaming?' I asked myself.

'You must be thrilled about the photo shoot tomorrow,' I said as I put Pat's tea on the table at his side.

'By golly, I am! I'll be up early to press my uniform, brush my cap and polish my boots. Then I'll wash and shave before setting off for the posh hotel.'

I smiled at the thought of Pat shaving. What exactly would he shave? His neck? Face? I was intrigued!

'They're sending a taxi for me at nine,' he continued, excitement etched on his face.

I opened my mouth to speak and the hall clock began striking ten.

'By 'eck! I must be off! I need my beauty sleep.' Another sideways smile.

We said farewell at the door and I wished Pat all the best for the next day. As he left, I *swear* he was humming the Postman Pat theme tune under his breath and I watched with disbelief as he disappeared into the night.

November 2000: *I was saddened to read that my friend, Postman Pat, had been given the sack. Royal Mail said the cheery delivery man, whose good name had done so much to promote the services of the organisation, had been dumped because he no longer fitted in with the company's corporate image. The Postal Workers' Union described the decision as a disgrace.*

Eric Sprat

Pat Sibbons

Eric liked 'em large. That was a fact. One of his earliest memories was staring across his grandma's front room at Auntie Norah. Norah sat between his skinny grandma and his even skinnier mother. Sitting on the floor opposite the sofa, he'd had a clear view straight up Auntie Norah's skirt. *What was that?* he'd wondered. He had wriggled his little bottom closer. None of the adults had taken any notice of him. They were laughing and smoking and drinking Mackeson. Now he had a clearer view. A roll of marshmallow pink fat oozed out from the top of her stockings. As she chuckled, her enormous bosoms bounced up and down. Exquisite. He didn't know the word at that time but that was the thought that formed in his head as he stared.

Eric popped into the Sunlight Café on his way to work every morning. He bought a cheese and pickle roll, ready salted crisps and a milky coffee for his lunch. Eric liked routine and order.

On this particular Monday morning there was someone different behind the counter. Immediately he spotted her he felt his heart begin to race.

'Can I help you?' said the vision of loveliness.

'Er, yes. Can I have a cheese and pickle roll, brown pickle not yellow, and a milky coffee to takeaway please?'

'Crusty or a bap?' asked the angel.

Maureen, the owner, appeared from the kitchen.

'Morning, Eric. I see you've met our new girl. This is Tracey. Tracey, this is Eric, one of our best customers. Eric will have a crusty roll.'

Tracey turned round to slice open the roll and Eric had a 360 degree view of the goddess before him. Her dark hair fell almost to her waist. It had no body to it at all. It hung in what his mother called 'rat-tails' and looked like it needed a good wash. Eric could forgive this imperfection in her as, where her hair finished, the hugest bottom he had ever seen began. Gargantuan. Vast. Epic.

Disappointingly, Tracey turned back towards him with the completed lunch order. Her blue eyes sat deep amongst the pale fleshiness of her face. Her chins were legion and there wasn't even a hint of a cheek bone. The buttons on her overall strained to contain the mountain of gorgeousness that it held within.

'Six pounds twenty, please.'

Eric handed over the cash in a daze.

He could think of nothing else but Tracey all day at work. As he nibbled his crisps he imagined feeding crisps to Tracey. *A family size bag of flaming steak and onion*, he thought. He would feed them in slowly, enjoying the look of ecstasy on her face as she crunched the fried potatoes to a pulp.

The next morning, Eric made a particular effort to look

good. This wasn't easy as sartorially elegant was not a description one could apply to him. He combed his thinning hair, splashed on some aftershave from the bottle gathering dust on the bedside cabinet and put on his best clothes. He looked at himself in the mirror in the spare room. A skinny, dishevelled, middle-aged man stared back at him. 'Perfect,' he said cheerfully as he left for the Sunlight.

He hesitated before he pushed open the door, smoothing down his hair and brushing dandruff from his shoulders. There she was, buttering toast. He pushed the door open before his courage left him.

'Morning, Tracey. Isn't it a lovely day?'

'Morning, erm?'

'Eric, it's Eric.'

'Oh yeah, Eric. I'll be right with you.'

He watched as she moved from behind the counter to serve poached eggs on toast to a customer. She truly was perfect. Every step she took looked like an effort. Her breath laboured from carrying the plate a few metres. Fantastic. He looked at her pudgy hands. No ring. Hopeful. After depositing the breakfast she slowly returned behind the counter.

'Crusty cheese roll with brown pickle and a milky coffee?'

She had remembered! He watched her as she worked, enjoying every straining motion she made.

'Six pounds twenty, please.'

Eric stood looking at the vision before him.

'Was there something else you'd like?' said Tracey

looking wary.

'Just your number.'

'Are you taking the mickey?'

'I am 100 per cent genuine, Tracey. I would very much like to take you out for a drink or a meal. I'd like to get to know you.'

Tracey laughed. 'But we would look odd together. Anyway, I don't eat out.'

'Why not?' said Eric.

'I find people watch me. They want to see what I'm eating and how much.'

'Well, why don't you come round to my place and I'll cook for you. What do you like to eat?'

Tracey hesitated. He looked okay and Maureen said he was alright. *Why not?* she thought. She'd only had one boyfriend and that had been years ago. Maybe, at last, her luck with men was about to change.

'Alright then, but I don't eat anything fancy or too foreign.'

Eric was thrilled and his face showed it. He wrote down his address and arranged for Tracey to come for supper the next night at 7.00 pm.

He called in sick the following day as he needed time to ensure everything would be perfect for his date. He spent the morning food shopping and, after lunch, set about preparing cottage pie and trifle. He browned the mince and drained off a little of the excess beef fat, only a little though. He then added onions and stock and let it simmer. Nothing additional was needed. *Just keep it simple*, he thought to himself. Then he made the mash. He added a huge dollop of Anchor butter, salt, pepper and double cream to make it extra tasty. After assembling meat and mash he finished off the dish with an enormous mound of mild cheddar. It looked delicious.

The trifle was made of an abundance of full-fat custard, jam-smeared sponge fingers and double cream. No fruit was added to sully the lusciousness of the dessert apart from a single, shiny glacé cherry on top.

At 7.10 pm the doorbell rang. Eric was ridiculously excited at the prospect of entertaining the beautiful Tracey in his own home. He opened the door and was not disappointed by the vision standing on his doorstep. Tracey had made an effort to look good for him. Her hair was held back from her face with a glittering Alice band and she was wearing grey eyeshadow and bright pink lipstick. He thought that it made her look like a cherub.

'Come in. Let me take your coat.' The coat was removed to reveal a sparking tunic top and black leggings. The top was vast but still didn't manage to contain that amazing derrière.

Going through to the lounge, Eric asked if she would like a drink before dinner.

'I don't drink alcohol. It tastes horrible. Have you got any Pepsi? The real stuff, not that awful-tasting, diet muck.'

Eric was in love. Tracey was all he wanted in a woman. He did have full-fat Pepsi and happily poured her a large glass in the kitchen, adding an extra teaspoon of sugar for luck.

After drinks, Eric seated Tracey at the dining table. She

was only just able to fit on the chair. *No worries*, he thought, *that can be easily rectified*. He brought the main course to the table. He had loaded his plate with a huge portion but had deliberately given Tracey a much smaller one. In his experience, larger ladies didn't want to appear greedy. He placed a bowl of carrots and peas on the table too. They probably wouldn't get eaten but they looked colourful.

The meal was a great success. Tracey said that the trifle was amazing and happily tucked into seconds. After dinner they talked for hours. They had a lot in common (Eric made sure they did) liking the same TV programmes, films and music. Like him, Tracey lived alone and had hardly any family to speak of. Just before midnight, Tracey said she had better go home as she had work in the morning. Eric called her a cab and helped her struggle into her coat.

'Can I see you again, Tracey? I've had such a lovely evening.'

'Me too,' said Tracey. 'Yes, that would be very nice.'

Eric gave her a delicate peck on her baby soft cheek and walked her out to the cab.

'I'll pop into the shop tomorrow as usual and we can organise something then.'

He closed the front behind him, satisfied with how things had gone. He walked up the stairs to the master bedroom with its super king bed and pretty, floral bed linen. No mirrors lined the walls or wardrobes, just a 70 inch plasma TV screen on the wall opposite the bed. Just perfect for anyone who was going to be spending the rest of their life in bed!

Time

Trisha Todd

I watch you now and wonder,
Where did all those years go?
You were just a babe in arms,
And passing years were slow.
I woke to find you fully grown,
My babe no more, your life your own.
I miss small arms around my neck,
The wet kiss pressed against my cheek.
Your soft, small hand in mine, held tight,
Your joyful face, your smile so bright.
Your giggle, your laugh – sounds so dear.
When did those happy times disappear?
It surely can't be years since then,
I want to live them all again.
But no, my child, you're fully grown,
And have small children of your own.

Mrs Redman

Michele Hawkins

Jemima had seen it all before and it made her so sad. Mrs Redman was such a lovely old lady, full of smiles despite her obvious pain as she ushered Jemima into her home. Jemima often wondered how she would cope if she found herself living alone with only an old radio and the daily visit by the carer for company.

I'd go stark raving mad, she thought to herself as she struggled out of her warm, navy blue duffel coat to reveal her sugar pink nylon uniform, completed with a pair of sturdy black lace-up shoes on top of thick woollen tights. Jemima grimaced; she really hated her uniform, clashing as it did with her fiery auburn hair. Today she wore her hair scraped back off her face in a bun, trying in vain to contain the springy curls which kept escaping.

'Do sit down, dear,' said Mrs Redman, 'and let me tell you all about Humphrey.'

Oh good, thought Jemima. *One of Mrs Redman's imaginary friends.* She had many and mostly they were remarkably interesting. In fact, Jemima didn't know for sure if any of the people Mrs Redman regaled her with tales of were actual people she had met or figments of her imagination, but either way it didn't bother her as she relished hearing about them.

Before making herself comfortable, Jemima whizzed around Mrs Redman's flat, making sure everything was shipshape. Satisfied all was in order, Jemima made them both a cup of tea. Placing the dainty cup and saucer in front of the kindly lady, she flopped into the armchair opposite and looked up expectantly.

Closing her deep green eyes, Mrs Redman took a deep shuddering breath. She wished the pain would go away but reasoned, at her age, it was a small price to pay. Retrieving a lacy hankie from the sleeve of her fawn-coloured jumper, she dabbed her eyes as she thought of Humphrey. Not for the first time she wondered if she should burden this young girl with her secret but over time they had developed a comradeship and she now felt sure Jemima could cope. Folding her hands neatly in her lap, and with mind made up, she began the story. Jemima listened, totally engrossed.

'I was fifteen when I first met Humphrey. It was a few years after the end of the Second World War. Times were still hard but the mood had changed, optimism was in the air. It scooped up and carried even the most reticent. I loved him at first sight. Older than me, he had just turned eighteen. He seemed worldly wise, exciting, exotic even with his slicked back dark hair and long, tapering fingers always caressing a cigarette. He mesmerised me. I'd led a sheltered life, the much longed-for only child, which meant I spent most of my time in a bubble of three. My grandparents had either already passed away or did so before my second birthday and so I had absolutely no recollection of them.

'We became friends but as soon as I turned sixteen it developed into a relationship. Our first kiss was so tender, my heart felt as if it would surely stop.'

'How romantic,' breathed Jemima.

'My parents trusted Humphrey. He came from 'the good part' of London, which basically meant his family was wealthy, respected. Very quickly we became inseparable. Humphrey was working for his family business, an export company, doing extremely well now trade across the world had opened up again. The wedding took place shortly after my eighteenth birthday, my beautiful dress a birthday present from my parents. It was new and made of satin covered in delicate antique lace.

'We moved into a small flat near his work and began married life. He used to say that when our children come along, we'd move into a house. Sadly, we were not blessed with children and, looking back, this was the start of our problems.

'We moved into this house as Humphrey said it was expected of someone in his position to have somewhere to entertain important clients when they visited London from abroad. It was soulless, though, with no children's excitable chatter to break the silence.

'At first I enjoyed making our house comfortable, choosing fabrics and furnishings, preparing a hot meal for when Humphrey came home. I wasn't allowed to work. I accepted this without question but occasionally suggested becoming involved with a local women's group to ease my daytime loneliness. Humphrey made it clear that he wanted me to be available for him; he didn't want to share me. When my parents, suddenly and shockingly, died in a car crash he held me, and comforted me, but as life gradually returned to a semblance of normality, I realised I'd been distant from my parents in recent years and I had no friends of my own. Humphrey had effectively isolated me, little by little, and I hadn't noticed.

'That night, I made him his favourite dinner and watched him eat it as I was too upset to feel hungry. He didn't appear to notice. When exactly had things changed? I gave an involuntary shiver as I acknowledged the emotion I was feeling. It was fear. I dreaded upsetting him. I had spent my whole marriage tiptoeing around him, always aware of what mood he was in. The physical side of our relationship happened only when Humphrey felt like it. My needs were never considered. After I had cleared up, I took him a cup of coffee into the lounge where he was sitting, flicking through the paper. He didn't even glance at me let alone thank me as I placed the cup and saucer on the table beside his armchair. Well, something inside me switched on. Instead of my carefully thought out conversation that I'd practised all day, I shouted at him. All my pent-up emotions came tumbling out.

'Then the most frightening thing happened. There was total silence as he coldly looked me up and down. He told me he was seeing his secretary and had been for the last five years. I was surplus to requirements and he was going to sort it out. I expected to be devastated but instead I felt relieved. I was going to be free of this life. He was so matter of fact, hardly looking at me as he listed my faults, each one a blow as if physical.

'Eventually, I couldn't listen anymore; I was overwhelmingly tired, beaten down by his bullying. I summoned as much strength as I could and walked out of the lounge towards the stairs. I didn't know how I was going to be able to climb them as my legs were shaking uncontrollably. Suddenly, I felt his breath on my neck and his hands snaked around my throat. He was strong, I was weak. It was over in a matter of minutes. I guess you're wondering how he disposed of my body aren't you?'

Jemima made a funny noise in her throat. Mrs Redman took this as an affirmation and went on. 'Look in the garden, dear. See the plum tree? I'm buried under it.'

Pet Shop

Lois Maulkin

It's a young man's game this, really. Or a young person's I should say. Not that I'm that old. I'm not old enough to remember when people's animals came just as they were, as you might put it, though my dad remembers those times. Just. In his father's day, of course, if you wanted an animal to have a special talent or a particular look you had to breed it in. Took generations, it did, crossing this bitch with that dog, this ram with that ewe, hoping one of the offspring would be the colour you wanted, have the curl of horn, the softness of mouth, the plumpness, even temper, ferocity, whatever it was you were after. Then you'd cross that one with a similar one from another litter and hope you were strengthening, intensifying, the characteristic. Years it took. Dad remembers things starting to change. He remembers protest marches about it all, even though he was a small boy then and didn't join in. They never came to much, he said. I think once people realised how bloody convenient everything was about to become, they all just sat back to enjoy the show.

I look around the shop now. I'm proud of it, I'll admit. We've kept it very traditional, nostalgic even, with huge glass jars of sunflower seeds and millet on wooden shelves and big, waxy-looking bones heaped in baskets. We keep it smelling of warm hay. It's on the 'Back to the Land' app which also offers cut grass, flowering nettles, oxeye daisies at noon, sun-burnt farmhand, tractor exhaust, porker's poo and loads of other 'nature' smells but the warm hay is our signature scent. I say 'our' and 'we', but it's just me working here these days, making the decisions, really. Dad's, well, Dad's less involved now.

The mynah bird, in its rust-coloured cage hanging in the window, sings and chatters away all day so I'm not too lonely. And most nights I take the mynah bird home with me so I'm not lonely there, either. On the counter, in the old-fashioned way, is the Pick Book, open at a page that shows the latest small mammal options, sparkly rats being particularly eye-catching and a current bestseller.

Wednesday afternoon is never a busy time here, and I'm slumped in my high armchair, almost dozing, at the till. The animals are sleeping in their big pen which is white, about a foot high and has cream-coloured blankets in cosy heaps for the puppies, kittens, rabbits, ferrets, mice and guinea pigs to lay amongst. I've arranged them to look their most appealing, with their little paws tucked together. Sometimes I arrange them cuddling each other. Dad remembers a time when you couldn't have kept them all together like this but, thankfully, we can now. They won't wake up until they're needed and, anyway, they've all been sorted. It must have been a nightmare back in the old days when they all woke up whenever they wanted. I can't imagine it, all of them going to the toilet all over the place, making a racket and trying to eat each other. Who'd have opted to keep a pet in those times? Thank the Lord we're past all that now. Dad remembers his father saying there was a time when you'd maybe neuter an animal, worm it and give it a jab or two and that was it. Job done and off they'd go. Dad says it was all anyone wanted or expected. Hark at me, 'Dad says this, Dad remembers that.' I'm falling into reminiscence.

The shop door opens and a girl of about ten comes in followed by a woman I assume to be her mother. The woman has a round, ball-shaped head and a baby's face; smooth, plump, a creamy pink, with full, wet lips and one tiny tooth. Her short hair is blonde and wispy, so fine I can see her scalp through it. It sits in two or three small, soft curls high on her forehead. It is a fashionable look at the moment, about as young-looking as you can get without resembling a foetus. The girl has green ears like a sprite and long hair in lots of wide plaits woven round her body into a pinafore dress. They are a very stylish pair.

I come round the counter to greet them and realise I can hardly hear myself speak over the mynah bird, which is giving Enoch Powell's 'Rivers of Blood' speech for all it's worth. I shush it and it says, 'Sorry, Michael, I'll keep it down,' and carries on in a stage whisper. The little girl laughs and her mother smiles. I suggest it stops the hate-filled, archaic political rhetoric, please, and sings something pleasant instead.

'Your wish is my command, Michael,' it says, and begins to sing softly. After the usual pleasantries I say to the woman, 'So, what can I help you with today? A guinea pig that's also an alarm clock? A cat that changes colour and does the dishes? A handbag mouse that suggests ideal compliments for everyone you meet and counts your calories? Not that you need to watch your calories, obviously.' I catch the woman's eye and feel myself blushing. Oh dear God, I'm attracted to her. How inconvenient.

Either she hasn't noticed or she's super-cool or, most likely, totally disinterested but the woman says, 'You've been recommended to us. My mother died a few months ago and, among other things, she left her laugh to my daughter, Eve, here.'

'What a lovely way to remember her,' I say.

'Isn't it?' says the woman. Her voice is high and reedy. I feel my shoulder blades tingling as I hear it. 'And we'd like it put into a dog. Quite a large one, grey and smelling of lavender. Is that something you can help us with?'

I rub my hands together, realise I look slightly sinister and pull them apart. 'Yes,' I say. 'You've come to exactly the right place. That's just the kind of thing we specialise in. These are our dogs, amongst our other, top quality house pets.' I spread my arms to indicate the slumbering animals. 'Perhaps Eve would like to choose a puppy? Step in, go ahead. Feel free to stroke them, Eve, give them a bit of a squeeze, see which one you like the feel of. Don't worry about what colour it is or how large or small you think it might grow; we can tweak that kind of thing at the software stage. Just find one you think you'd like to have around, laughing like your grandmother.'

'And if you'd like to come this way, madam,' I wince at the formality and notice a blob of dribble spill across the woman's pursed cherub's lips down onto her chin. I feel an odd rush of excitement. Dad's always said I was too picky about women and that's why I've ended up on my own. 'Ended up'; I've not ended up. I'm only just beginning. Well, that's how I feel. Okay, maybe I'm halfway there but I've not 'ended up' anything. I can't quite believe I'm thinking it but this feels almost like some sort of beginning. My excitement builds.

'And this is the Pick Book, which lists our extensive options, many of which are not available anywhere else,' I say, trying not to sound too grand. Off-putting. Turning to the page marked 'Pick Pooches' I let my fingers touch a selection of seven or eight icons which light up.

'Can I get you a chair and a cup of tea? Or a glass, or bottle, of milk?' I say, 'so you can take your time and relax while you're making your choices?'

'Thank you, no, I don't have long. Perhaps you could just quickly outline the various options for me, please? Unless it's a bit of a cheek to ask?' she says. I notice she lisps ever so slightly. My knees tremble.

'That's no trouble at all; it's what I'm here for,' I say, standing next to her and noticing the smell of her perfume. It is the currently very fashionable 'Lotion Bebe'. She wears an over-size dummy on a pink satin ribbon round her neck and pops it into her mouth as I start describing what's on offer. The mynah bird has grown loud again and is singing 'Come On Baby Light My Fire', and I feel embarrassed and shush it. The bird takes no notice and I give it a grim look. It looks grimly back and sings on, gyrating its hips.

'So, basically,' I begin, and go on to describe every available nuance of lavender-smelling grey dog with an old woman's laugh that we can offer. We go fairly briskly through the standard breeds then on to bespoke animals, length of leg, tail options, texture and fullness of coat, shape of muzzle. Then the smell; English lavender, French lavender, Sicilian or bath salts. And colour; winter afternoon, ash, dove, London sky, ghost ship and thirty-seven other shades of grey. Is the dog to be a guard dog, a family pet, a lapdog, a hunter, a ratter, a performer? The laugh can be constant, instead of a bark or a growl. It can occur only when the dog is actually amused, which is not a big ask if you're going with the dog's natural sense of humour but, as this is not something usually terribly well developed, it would probably necessitate installing a humanoid sense of humour. And then you get into whether you'd like it to be a generic sense of humour, or a similar sense of humour to the grandmother. In which case, has the grandmother's sense of humour ever been downloaded anywhere? Perhaps, ahem, by the police? And if not, can you describe that sense of humour?

'Or, and this might be nice,' I say, 'you could have Eve's sense of humour replicated and put in the dog so it laughs at things Eve would find funny.'

'I like that idea,' says the woman excitedly, letting her dummy fall out of her mouth. I gasp as it leaves her wet lips.

'Sorry?' she says

'Just a bit of a cough,' I say, reddening again.

The mynah bird's blasting away with 'Sugar Baby Love' now and I'm shocked by its spite.

'Forgive the mynah bird, please,' I smile at the woman. 'It has a penchant for antique songs.'

The woman politely brushes away my apology and gets back to the dog's sense of humour.

'It's a sweet touch. Would it diminish Eve's sense of humour, though, using it in a dog? Or harm her in any way?'

'Not at all,' I say, flapping my hand at the mynah bird. 'Sorry about this. No, it wouldn't hurt Eve at all, no more than taking a photograph of her would do. She won't even know it's happening; we can map it through her phone.'

'And is that a popular choice?' asks the woman, 'installing the owner's sense of humour?'

'It is, yes. Just last week I put someone's sense of humour into a woodpecker. It told several very successful 'knock knock' jokes shortly after.'

The woman laughs at my feeble attempt at wit and I feel I'm melting inside.

A door at the back of the shop opens and a Shetland pony walks in, says, 'It's three-thirty, boss, three-thirty everybody,' turns and trots out again.

'Then I haven't got long,' says the woman. 'So, to recap, when Eve's chosen a puppy, you upload a...a...what?'

'We upload a genetic template that will make the puppy grow, as we've discussed, into a large, gentle-natured bitch, with long legs and a shiny two-tone coat, in Autumn City and Dove Grey. She will have long hair which curls like a vintage perm on top of her head, and melting brown eyes with white visible round the iris. It's a small detail but it makes the whole face so much more expressive.' I hope I'm not showing off. 'And a long muzzle that is still wide enough to show when she is smiling. She will smell of English lavender, particularly after a shower of rain. There will be a four-inch square patch of Henniman's Tack-Proof Hard Hair on her chest where one or more of your late mother's brooches can be pinned.

'All our animals come ready prepared with a Pet U Like receptor which means they arrive with you non-moulting, non-aggressive, house trained and obedient. We can turn that off if you choose?' I look into her blue eyes, shining from their slits of fat.

'Oh no, we want all that, please.'

I smile and say, 'Very sensible,' conscious that the mynah bird has stopped singing and is beginning a husky rendition of 'Shall I Compare Thee to a Summer's Day?'.

'And using the Pet U Like receptor we will install Eve's sense of humour which the device will map and upload through her phone. It's an ongoing process which will allow for changes to Eve's sense of humour as she grows up. Then we upload your mother's laugh, which I believe you said you have stored on your key ring. The handset will, of course, have volume control.'

'Very important,' puts in the woman.

'Very important indeed,' I chuckle. I feel she is warming to me and the dull afternoon is suddenly full of golden twinkles. 'It all takes about five minutes, ten at the most, and then she'll be ready to take away.' I stop speaking abruptly, suddenly aware that this woman, this gorgeous massive baby, will shortly walk out of the shop and out of my life. I'm desperate to postpone that moment for as long as possible. While we're still talking, something might happen. And I want it to. I definitely want it to. My wanting makes me bold. 'Or I can deliver her personally, distance no object.'

The woman hesitates briefly. 'That would be very convenient. We have a couple more errands this afternoon, and rather than carry the puppy round the town it would be good to have her taken home directly.'

'Or,' conscious I'm going out on a bit of a limb, 'you could run your errands while I do the install, and then I could give you two a lift back with the dog in my car. Which I'll be in too. Erm. Driving.'

The woman considers this, her mouth a wet rosebud pout and her head on one side. It feels as though time is hanging hot and fizzy, in a late-summer-haze kind of way, while I wait for her reply.

Tension mounts within me. I'm willing her to say yes.

'It must be love, love, love...' bawls the mynah bird and suddenly, unthinking, I snarl and flash it a murderous look.

The woman hears and sees. She flinches. Her chin quivers and her blue eyes fill with tears and one of us, I'm not sure if it is her or me, lets out a sort of strangled yelp. A gargle, if you will, of despair. If there has been any spell in the air it is broken now.

She says, 'No, thank you, we'll take her now. She'll

95

sleep in my shopping bag until we're home. Eve, hurry up and choose so the man can do the install and we can get on.'

She pops her dummy back into her fat cherub's mouth and once Eve has picked out a sleek, snoring puppy, I set up and install the necessary. It doesn't take more than four or five minutes and during that time the woman watches a troupe of dancing mega-bacteria on her phone.

I wrap the puppy and its handset in perforated brown paper tied with string, my fingers fumbling with the knots embarrassingly. Eventually, I hand over the parcel, saying, 'Full instructions are on the handset, and–' but the woman busies herself putting the parcel into her bag, making a point of not listening, and I stop talking.

She says, 'Very helpful. Thank you,' almost coldly, and blinks at the till which says 'Kerching! Thank you so much, do call again'.

Miserably, I hold the door open and close it behind them as they leave.

'Ah dear,' says the mynah bird, bobbing up and down on its perch. 'You messed that up, didn't you?'

As a familiar cloak of despondency falls over me, I look at the bird, trapped for years in its rusty cage, its shining black feathers and bright beak glinting. *It is a nasty piece of work*, I think. *Vicious*.

'Shut up, Dad,' I say.

Castles in the Sand

Sue Duggans

She sat by a rock pool, concealed. Golden hair, lifted intermittently by the breeze, cascaded over her shoulders. The sun was warm and, with beauty and suspicion etched on her salt-streaked face, she surveyed the expansive beach and green-blue sea.

Far off, matchstick people arrived in clusters. Some moved her way but it was a trudge when weighed down with the paraphernalia of beach outings and small children.

As the sun climbed, its heat intensified. She slipped into the coolness of the rock pool sending crabs scurrying, fearing for their lives. A daring seagull, bead eye transfixed on lunch, circled and landed nearby then, alarmed by her unexpected yet graceful movement, flew off.

A family settled overly-close but seemed too absorbed in themselves to be worried about her. She was out of view but, by moving this way and that, could observe them through gaps in haphazardly-placed rocks. The bronzed mother wore large yellow-framed sunglasses and an outfit, not unlike her own in colour, which shimmered in the sunlight. She found the father's naked muscular torso, like that of a swimmer, attractive. Two excited children, a boy and a girl, chased each other and rolled in the sand, resembling excited puppies. The sun, still hot, required them to have cream smeared over their faces and limbs which they objected to vociferously.

'It's important. Mummy knows best.' The father said very little but spoke with authority. The girl dropped her head and became hushed but the boy continued to complain. In no time it was done. The boy occupied himself by building towers of stones then knocking them down repeatedly with a ball. The girl took a bucket and spade and built castles in the sand. She was totally engrossed constructing a circle of little sandcastles, persevering when one collapsed and had to be rebuilt. Circle completed, the girl wandered around gathering adornments for her creation – shells, stones, sticks washed up by the tide. She placed them with care on the little castles and smiled with approval then was off again searching for beach treasure.

Suddenly, she was standing there, by the rock pool, and their eyes met. The little girl's mouth was open in astonishment and her eyes shone like diamonds. From her place on the rocks, and through drapes of golden hair, she raised a finger to her lips pleading for secrecy. The girl nodded in consent and smiled beautifully then, eyes transfixed, bent down and picked up strands of seaweed.

'Matilda! Matilda! We must leave in five minutes. It's piano at four.' The girl turned and raced away clutching seaweed. Departing, feet heavy, the little girl turned and gave a discreet wave then was gone.

The sun was dipping and the tide advancing at pace as she shuffled uncomfortably and prepared herself then, at the right moment, glided from the rocks and into the sea. Disappearing beneath the waves, the rays from the setting sun shone on silvery scales. Then, with a final flip of her tail, she was gone!

No Room for Escape

Pat Sibbons

Drip, drip, drip! She could hear water over to her left. Where was she? Her head throbbed and she felt so incredibly tired she couldn't open her eyes. She drifted back to sleep, for how long she didn't know.

Drip, drip, drip! The sound woke her again. Her head felt like a nail was being driven into her eye but she managed to prise her eyelids apart. She struggled to focus. Shapes and colours merged into each other. Jumbled up images slowly came into focus. The ceiling was covered in old-fashioned white tiles. Without a window, there was no natural light but a lone, bare light bulb dangled above her dimly. Turning her head was painful but she managed to look towards the sound. An orange sink unit. The handle of a filthy frying pan poked up like an iceberg from murky water as a limescale-encrusted tap dripped. Above, a camera peered down at her. A clock next to it said it was 4.20 pm. She turned her head slowly to the other side. A grimy wall cupboard. An old, pine dresser, bare apart from a floral cup and saucer, a pack of cards and a soft white rabbit. Next to it was a door. Where on earth was she?

She tried to sit up but couldn't move. Her hands crept across her body. Plastic straps held her down. She felt around her. She was on a table. Her mind raced as panic mounted. She was trapped, where and by whom she had no idea. She tried to struggle free but the straps didn't move an inch.

How had she ended up here? No memories were coming. Who was she? Where did she live? She didn't remember anything before hearing that dripping tap. Warm tears ran down her cheeks and pooled in her ears. She stared up at the light bulb.

Footsteps. Someone was coming. She had to move. She pulled desperately at the straps but they held firm. A key turned in the lock. She closed her eyes.

The door opened and someone approached the table.

'I know you are awake; I've been watching you. I've been waiting for you to wake up. It's up to you whether you pretend to be asleep but the outcome will be the same.' Her captor was female.

She could hear the woman walking around the table, breathing heavily. Terrified but curious, she opened her eyes. The woman stood at her feet. Hands behind her back. She wore a black boiler suit and Queen of Hearts mask.

'Why am I here? What do you want?' she managed to say. Her throat felt dry and sore.

The woman didn't reply. She brought her right hand around in front of her. She was holding a machete. The metal sparkled in the light from the bulb above.

She let out a low wail at the sight of the weapon. She was going to die, here in this filthy kitchen.

The woman slowly raised the machete above her head.

She turned and pointed at the clock on the wall.

'I will give you until 5.15 to escape. If you are still in this room then, this beautiful, shiny object will part your head from your body. In the unlikely event you manage to get out, I won't come after you and you will be safe.'

The masked woman walked back to the door, opened it and said, 'You only have fifty minutes so I would get on with it if I were you.'

As the key turned in the lock she arched her back, trying to break the straps. They held fast. After a couple of minutes she lay still to think. She had to cut the straps. She felt in the front pockets of her jeans. It was tight but she managed to pull out a plaster and a tissue. Useless! It was 4.40 pm.

She ran her right hand along the edge of the table. Just smooth wood. She tried the other side and, just below the edge, she felt a handle. There was a drawer. She managed to open it a couple of inches and thrust her hand inside. Snap! The pain as the mouse trap came down on her fingers was incredible. Screaming, she withdrew her hand, pulling off the trap and flinging it against the wall.

As the pain subsided a little, she tentatively put her hand back in the drawer. She moved her hand around like a spider. Nothing. She screamed in frustration. Putting her hand back in, this time she worked around the sides from front to back. As her hand passed the left edge it crossed something cold and sharp. She cried out as the knife cut into her palm. She tried to free it but it was stuck to the side of the drawer. She tugged and wriggled the knife and, with a huge effort, managed to pull it out. Her hand and the knife were covered in blood but she didn't pause as she sawed at the straps that bound her.

At 4.50 pm, the final strap fell away. She sat up, throwing the straps on the floor. What now? She stood up on legs that felt like teabags tied together with string. She had heard the door lock but went over nevertheless and tried the handle. The woman had challenged her to escape and so it must be possible. She looked around. One locked door. No windows. She opened the cupboard. It was empty. She checked the dresser. Nothing there except some tat and a stupid stuffed rabbit. She picked it up and chucked it against the wall. Thud! It had something in it. She picked it up. It was definitely heavier than it looked. She grabbed the knife and cut through the stitches along its back. Desperately, she pulled out the stuffing and found a key. The relief made her sink to the floor. Pulling herself together she ran to the door, still carrying the knife in case the woman was waiting for her on the other side. She inserted the key in the lock; freedom was only seconds away. It wouldn't turn. She tried again but it wasn't the right key. It was 5.00 pm.

She sat with her back against the door. She would fight when the time came. The knife looked pathetic against the machete but she would fight. She looked at the key lying in her injured hand. If the key wasn't for this door, where was it for? She must have missed something. She opened the cupboard and the dresser. There was nothing there. She went over to the sink unit. Dropping to her knees she opened the doors. It was dark in there. She leant right in and felt around. Nothing! Frantically, she moved her hand across the back panel. There was something there. A memory flashed through her mind. *I am Megan Jones. I'm twenty-six. I'm a teacher.* It was a keyhole. She used her left hand to guide the key into the lock. Footsteps came towards the room. She turned the key in the tiny door and it opened. The key was being inserted into the other lock as she crawled on her stomach out of the room.

She was in a white room. A couch with huge soft cushions sat against one wall. On an ornate carved table there was a tray with a jug of ice-cold water and a crystal tumbler. A note on the tray said 'Congratulations! You are free. Please drink me.' She was so thirsty. Hesitating for just a second, she poured herself a glass of the cool liquid. She drank it down greedily. It tasted so good. She was exhausted. She had to get out of here but she didn't think she was physically capable of moving another inch. She flopped down onto the couch, thinking she would rest for a few minutes.

'Megan. Megan. How are you feeling?'

She opened her eyes. She was still lying on the couch. A woman looked down at her. She recognised the voice and recoiled in fear.

'Oh dear. Maybe you just need some more water. There should be enough restorer in there. You should have your memory fully back by now.' She handed her the glass. 'Just drink a little more.'

Megan stared at the woman as her mind began to refill. *I'm Megan Jones, I'm twenty-six. I'm a teacher and I asked for an extreme escape room experience for my birthday.*

105

Suicide Watch

Kim Kimber

Claire patrols the cliff, watching, vigilant. A crisp, autumnal chill hangs in the air, reducing the number of dog walkers and sightseers. It has been a quiet night so far. She has spoken to a couple of tourists, warned off some kids about cycling too close to the edge and nodded at passing shift workers as they hurry home.

She hears him before she sees him. Her trained ears catch a sound in a lull in the wind, the cry of the desperate. He is standing close to the cliff edge, peering down uncertainly at the perilous drop below.

'Hey,' she calls softly, her voice a whisper in the wind.

He ignores her, locked in his pain.

'Hey,' she says more loudly. 'Do you need help?'

He turns slightly, unable to see Claire through teary eyes.

'Go away,' he says gruffly. Long, matted, unkempt hair surrounds his face which, under different circumstances, would be handsome.

'I'd rather stay, if that's alright,' she says. 'I can see you are unhappy. It might help to talk.'

'Leave me alone...go home.'

'I don't have anywhere else to be so I'll stay if you don't mind.'

He looks down again and leans forward slightly. For a moment Claire thinks she has lost him but he falters. She fights the urge to reach out to him and instead wills him back from the edge.

'Why don't we sit and talk, I'm Claire. And you are..?'

He remains where he is, distracted, the demons in his head fighting against the words of the softly-spoken girl. Claire sits.

'Leave me be, go away,' he hisses.

'As I told you, there's nowhere I need to be. I can see you're hurting; it might help to talk.'

He shakes his head, wavering between relief and terror as he peers over the cliff down to the unforgiving rocks beneath. He is young, maybe in his early twenties, and inadequately dressed for the cold October night.

'What's your name?' she persists gently.

'John.'

'Hi John, I'd like to get to know you.'

'No, you wouldn't. No one likes me.'

'I'm sure that's not true.'

He sways precariously. Claire can feel his pain as though it was her own.

'John,' she says as gently as the wind allows. 'Please step away from the edge. Just for a moment. I'd really like to chat.'

'I just want it to end.'

'I'm sorry you feel like that but you're not alone. I'm here for you.'

'You don't know me.'

'But I'd really like to.'

'I'm a failure.'

'Could you tell me what has happened to make you so unhappy.'

'I flunked university, now I can't get a job, my parents think I'm useless and my girlfriend has left me. I just want it to stop.'

'Are you thinking of ending your life, John?'

He nods.

'I understand; I've felt like that too. You may not believe it now but your feelings will change.'

He hovers indecisively. 'It's the only way out.'

Claire shakes her head. 'There's always another way, John. I can help you if you'll let me. Let's sit and talk for a while.'

He steps back a little, nearer to Claire, then considers his actions. For a moment she thinks he is going to propel himself forward and leap off the cliff face. Instead, he takes another step back and sits in front of Claire with his back to her.

'I felt like you do now, a long time ago,' she says. 'I wanted to end my life but I now know that there are people who can help. That's why I patrol the cliffs, to seek out others who are suffering.'

John puts his head in his hands and sobs but she senses a slight change in him. Enough maybe to prevent him from jumping.

'Is there anyone I can call?'

He shakes his head. 'No one. Nobody cares.'

'It may feel like that, people say and do things they don't mean all the time. Maybe the people who are close to you don't realise how bad you're feeling.'

'My mum, you can call my mum,' he says eventually. He reaches into his pocket, takes out his mobile and brings up the number before passing it back to Claire.

She puts the phone to her ear. It never gets any easier. 'Hi, my name is Claire, you don't know me but I'm a friend of your son, John...no, he won't have mentioned me, we've only met recently...no I'm not from university. He's not feeling so well right now, could you come and collect him? He's a bit upset and doesn't want to talk but if you can come quickly...that's good. Where are you? I'll send you directions.'

The phone goes dead and Claire pushes the device back towards John. 'Your mum is on the way.'

He continues to sit with his back to her and the words tumble out, falteringly at first but then more forcibly...Claire sits and listens and nods. John is talking...there is no need for her to say any more. Her job is done.

A short while later, his flow of words is interrupted by a tap on the shoulder.

'John, what on earth, were you going to–? Oh my God, let's get you home. You must be frozen.'

John stands and faces his mum, allowing himself to be drawn into a hug. They both have tears in their eyes.

'Where is she?' he says, eventually.

His mum looks confused. 'Who? There's no one else here.'

'Claire, the girl who called you.'

'What girl? No one called. I was worried when you didn't come home. I had a sense that something was wrong. I felt pulled towards your room, as if something was guiding me. Your laptop was open at the page showing this location and, well, you've been so depressed lately, I came looking for you. Thank God I did. Nothing is that bad, son.'

A few weeks later, John returns, this time walking along the beach. On this occasion, it is daylight and he is dressed in long denim shorts and a crisp shirt. He smiles as the sun beams down. He lays a single red rose at the base of the cliff. 'Rest in peace, Claire,' he says. 'Thank you.'

Sleeping With the Enemy

Barbara Sleap

La Ferme de Fresnois had been commandeered as a billet for Nazi German soldiers as they worked blocking bridges in the area of Sarthe. Francine had dreaded their arrival and had only been given a short time to prepare her three spare rooms. But after the first week she was surprised by their politeness and general behaviour. The young men, Heinrich, Karl and Otto, all fair haired and blue eyed, had kept the rooms tidy and were very undemanding, unlike some of the young men she'd heard stories about from other residents of Fresnay.

Life was not easy though as she now had only a skeleton staff to tend the small farm. A local man, Guy, maintained the precious apple orchard and made cider. He also tended the vegetable patch and fruit trees from which Francine made jams and pickles to sell at market. She made bread from flour mixed with ground chestnuts or whatever was available to make loaves. Then there was Eloise who helped in the house and had quickly learned to make goat's cheese. She had also become an expert on bees, looking after the three beehives that provided honey.

Francine was finding it hard to pay the meagre wages they relied on so much. She dreaded the thought of having to let one of them go as she took less and less to the once-thriving town market. Because of the soldiers, she now had three extra mouths to feed several days each week. The few stallholders felt intimidated by the Germans, some of whom demanded their goods at vastly lower prices.

Francine's husband, Jean-Paul, had been called on to fight for France as soon as the country entered the war. She had heard nothing for eighteen long months. The news wasn't good from the front either; the Germans had taken Paris and were rapidly moving further north. However, behind the scenes there was a small Maquis group in the neighbourhood that did their best to outwit the enemy in any way they could. Messages were sent by a hidden radio that was moved around the area as much as possible to prevent a signal being detected. Francine willingly played a small part. On certain days she was instructed to don a bright headscarf and walk around the farm once, twice and occasionally three times. She was aware this act sent a message to someone, she didn't know who, but someone was obviously watching. The farm sometimes became a haven for a few escaped allied airmen or soldiers who stayed overnight in the cellar beneath the house, which became more risky when her German guests arrived.

Francine sighed as she kneaded dough made from coarse flour and ground chestnuts; it had a strange flavour but was filling and better than nothing. This winter had crept up on her. Tomorrow was 'Le jour de Noel', so she intended to kill her oldest hen to make a stew for a treat, even though she would spend the day alone. She would make it last a few days too. Travel was restricted so she couldn't visit her sister, Paulette, who lived with her young family in St Paul on the other side of the river. You had to have a reason to cross and the papers she possessed only allowed her to cross once a week on market day.

Next day dawned, icy with a damp mist lying over the fields. But she still had her daily chores to perform. Yesterday, her 'guests' had cheerfully gone with their unit to the Hotel Le Grand Jardin in Mayenne for what would, no doubt, be two nights of music and drinking. After milking the goats, checking the bees and collecting eggs, Francine treated herself to one of the eggs, softly boiled and accompanied by a thick slice of bread. She was enjoying the peace and quiet as she sipped an elderflower tisane when she heard a creaking noise from above. Nervously, she climbed the stairs to investigate. The first room she peeped into was empty apart from clothes belonging to Heinrich, lying on the chair. She pushed open the door to the next room and gave a small shriek as she saw Otto lying fully clothed on the bed reading a book. He sat up quickly apologising for having disturbed her. Francine, still recovering from her shock, told him to come downstairs for coffee. He thanked her but said he didn't want to bother her and was quite content on his own. But Francine insisted; she had already lit the fire in the hearth and the bedroom was freezing.

Otto sat at the table and warmed his hands in front of the fire.

'Merci, Madame,' he said, smiling at Francine.

She smiled as Otto explained to her that he hadn't felt

like celebrating at the hotel with the others.

'They will drink too much and become too loud.'

He then told her he just needed some quiet time to think of his family who lived near Hamburg as did his fiancée, Lillian. No letters had been forthcoming from home in six months. Francine was able to sympathise as her first thought on waking each morning was of Jean-Paul. She put a cup of the bitter coffee, made from crushed acorns, in front of Otto, and he drank it gratefully.

'I miss Lillian so much,' he said.

For the next few hours they talked easily about their families, the war and their hopes for the future. She described her life on the farm and he told her about his work as a carpenter in Hamburg. He hadn't wanted to fight Hitler's war. He just wanted to marry Lillian, build their own house and raise a family.

Francine put a few extra logs on the little fire. It burned cosily as they moved from the table to the sagging sofa by the hearth. Otto's eyes filled as they discussed their views on the future of the two countries. He stroked Francine's hand as he spoke. She tried to pull away but he held on gently as he stroked her work-worn fingers. After a while, Francine opened a bottle of homemade cider which they drank silently, both caught up with their own thoughts.

The cider must have gone to Francine's head because she stumbled as she stood up to begin preparations for the stew. Otto caught her before she fell and, before they realised, they were in each other's arms. His steely blue eyes didn't leave her face and soon they were kissing, wildly and desperately, fired by loneliness and frustration. Just two people who had been starved of love and affection while the world outside continued its madness. The rest of the day they spent wrapped in each other's arms. They made love on the rug in front of the fire, blocking out all thoughts of war and the fact that they were on opposite sides.

'Tu es très belle,' Otto whispered in Francine's ear.

They ravenously devoured the scrawny chicken and, not wanting to sleep alone, climbed the stairs and slept soundly in Francine's bed, not letting go of each other all night.

As an icy dawn peeped through the shutters, Otto rose and left the house. Heinrich and Karl returned later in a boisterous mood which made Francine uneasy. She longed for Otto to return. He arrived later and was greeted loudly as the other two men regaled the events of the past nights; there was loud guffawing and backslapping as Otto listened. He caught Francine's eye and gave her a knowing little smile which she returned before quickly busying herself making breakfast.

After New Year, Otto's unit was replaced by another. Before he left, he and Francine managed to say a gentle and fond farewell but they both knew they wouldn't meet again. Their short Christmas romance would not be forgotten for the freedom and comfort it had given them. Something to remember, with hope, during the dreadful days that would surely follow.

The Counsellor

Michele Hawkins

My name is Ellie. I guess people see me as harmless. By that I mean even-tempered, approachable but professional. I'm not given to extremes of emotion. No wailing and gnashing of teeth for me. I have never lost control. Don't get me wrong, I do feel emotion, like when my brother, Paul, was diagnosed with cancer. I held him tightly while he sobbed, silent tears rolling down my face, as well as his, falling softly into his wavy, dark brown hair. Hair that he might have lost if chemo was required. Luckily, it wasn't.

This control is helpful as I make a living as a counsellor. I spend most of my days listening to a wide range of human tragedies. Loss is the most common. Loss of love or a loved one, loss of hope, loss of dignity. How to move on from loss; well, this is my bread and butter. Unfortunately, there is no magic pill and everyone reacts differently but, ultimately, any loss takes time to work through. We all have good days and bad days. The hope is eventually to have more good than bad.

My first client of the morning was Susan who had come to see me after her father had passed away. She was having difficulty understanding why she couldn't get over his death, her words not mine. She was in her thirties and married to Evan.

Our first session had been on a wet and windy Tuesday in January. The wind whipped around the buildings, chasing dead leaves and debris left by careless people. Occasionally, the rain hammered against the windows making the panes jump in shock, rattling to show their displeasure and age. I was still in the same rented room I'd found when I started my counselling business more than ten years previously. It was on the top floor of an old building in the town square, now hemmed in by the modern, glass-fronted monstrosities so prevalent in towns up and down the country.

Susan looked a little like me. Long dark hair, although mine was always neatly pinned into a bun, a professional look I felt. Hers was loose, teased into gentle waves that caressed her face and shoulders. She had a button nose whereas mine was more dominant, the same colour eyes, blue, and high cheekbones. We were also a similar dress size but she was always casually dressed whereas each morning I chose a below-the-knee skirt with a blouse from my impressive collection. Some days I felt bold and went for a brightly coloured blouse but mostly they were soft pastel shades, soothing.

That first meeting, Susan was dressed in a bright green jumper and denim jeans, artfully ripped on one knee, feet stuffed into a pair of burgundy Doc Martens. The first meeting is always about gaining trust. Some clients appear happy to talk, instantly forming a rapport, desperate to offload. I never took what they said as being the absolute truth though; it often took a couple of sessions or more to get to the heart of the issue. Susan, however, seemed reluctant to give away much about herself and the things she did share sounded strange somehow. However, as I have said, this is not unexpected. We had ended that first session by making an appointment for the following week despite Susan wanting to return as soon as possible. I don't generally make appointments more frequently than weekly as it's useful to allow the client to consider our discussion and begin the process that will eventually lead to acceptance. When Susan left, I had let out a long sigh; I felt as if I'd been holding my breath. Reflecting on the session it struck me why I'd felt tense. Susan had deflected questions and I realised that I'd given away far more about myself than I ever would normally.

***

I had been seeing Susan weekly for six weeks now and didn't feel that we were progressing. It was time to address this.

'Susan, perhaps we should decrease the sessions to once a fortnight.'

Her jaw tensed and, as I awaited her response, I noticed a tick at the corner of her left eye. Her knuckles were clenched tightly and, as I watched, they turned white. A pink flush pricked at her collarbone spreading upwards and, upon reaching her cheeks, two bright red spots appeared. But it was her eyes that shocked me. It was only a fleeting change but as she held my gaze, they appeared to turn an angry, glittery black before she blinked and they were blue again.

'Okay,' she said tightly, before getting up and striding towards the door. Her hand was on the handle before I could react.

'Wait a minute, Susan. We should discuss why that upset you.'

Totally ignoring me she left the room, slamming the door so hard behind her it rattled. I felt shaken. What had just happened? I was used to a range of emotions from my clients but this felt personal. I had been so busy lately that, despite noting down my discomfort about Susan's reactions, my mind had quickly turned to the next client after each session. I reread my notes and had to acknowledge we were not making progress. I decided to call Susan to suggest she saw another counsellor, someone I hoped could break through her defences, but she didn't answer her phone. Mentally noting to try again in the morning, I gathered up my belongings and strode out of my office. As I walked across the square to collect my dry cleaning, I had the strangest sense that I was being watched. Stopping, I slowly turned round on the spot. Nothing.

'Don't be silly, Ellie,' I muttered to myself. Shrugging off the feeling, I continued on. As I entered 'Philippa's Press' the bell tinkled announcing my arrival.

'Oh, hi Ellie, what can I do for you?' Philippa smiled.

'Hi, Phil, just popped in on the off chance my suits were ready.'

Philippa looked bemused. 'Susan collected them for you a short while ago. She said you'd asked her to.'

I must have looked puzzled as Philippa went on, 'Your

cousin Susan, Ellie!'

'What did she look like?' I replied with a growing sense of panic, my fears confirmed as Phil described my client, Susan.

'No problem,' I said backing out of the shop, the cheery bell grating my taut nerves. As I walked towards my car, I had to stop and take a few deep breaths to calm my racing heart.

When I reached my car, I let out a gasp of dismay. A deep jagged line was scored right along the driver's side of my lovely little Fiat 500. With shaking fingers, I found my keys and got into my car. Luckily, I only had a short drive home. The blood was pounding in my ears, drowning out the music from the radio.

Once settled in the lounge with a soothing cup of chamomile tea, I felt a little better and tried to think through events logically. Susan's behaviour had shaken me but all she'd actually done was pick up my dry cleaning. Odd, but a minor offence. Of course, I also suspected she had keyed my car but there wasn't any proof. I decided to report my suspicions to the police anyway.

A few weeks later and nothing untoward had happened. I hadn't heard from Susan, which was a relief, and I knew the police had spoken to her. My dry cleaning still hadn't turned up but I could live without a couple of suits. As I sat at the table savouring my breakfast of toast with generously spread creamy butter and real coffee percolated to perfection, the doorbell rang. It was the detective who had taken my statement.

'May I come in? I have some news about Susan.'

'Sure, come in and have a coffee.'

Once settled, slurping his coffee contentedly, the detective told me that Susan had been arrested and was on remand for murder. Not one but, so far, four murders. He explained that the case had been ongoing for a while.

'A serial killer, Susan?' I said in disbelief. 'She unsettled me when she was a client and she clearly had attachment and anger issues which is why I tried to refer her on for specialist help, but a murderer?'

The detective showed me pictures they'd taken in Susan's house. I couldn't take it in. My face was staring back at me from the walls of her bedroom; looking harassed, laughing while chatting with a friend outside the gym, on my phone outside my office, getting into my car at home. The pictures went on and on. The last one was of my suits hanging up in a wardrobe still in their clear plastic protectors.

'You were lucky,' the detective said, breaking into my bewildered silence. 'She took items of her victims' clothing shortly before murdering them.'

Every Cloud

Pat Sibbons

'Give him a little nudge with your toe.'

'I don't think so! I'm not kicking him!'

'I didn't say kick him, now did I? I said a little nudge, just to make sure he is dead.'

'Of course he's dead! Look at the colour of him!'

'Should we close his eyes at least?'

'You can if you want. I'm not touching him.'

Stuart and Stan stood side by side, staring down at the body on the lounge carpet.

'How do you think it happened?' asked Stan.

'Don't know. He wasn't that old really,' replied a frowning Stuart.

'I am surprised. You would have thought, in this day and age, with all this technology, that things like this wouldn't happen.'

'Yeah! You would, but the same thing happened to my mate Joe, from the allotments. He came home one afternoon and found his one face down in the kitchen. Pots boiling away.'

'See,' said Stan. 'There are safety implications. Imagine if he had come home later. The house could have burnt down.'

'His poor dog was going mental, apparently.'

'These innovations always seem like such a good idea, until things go wrong.'

The pair stood pondering the situation for a moment, not quite scratching their heads but something similar.

'So, what do we do now? Is there a number we have to call? There is a help line for day-to-day issues but I don't know what to do in a situation like this. I hope I'm not expected to dispose of him. My poor back isn't up to shifting him.' Stuart rubbed his lower back to indicate where the deficiency was.

'No,' said Stan, 'they can't expect you to sort this out. You are the victim here, mate. You are the one left without the service you have paid for. The customer is always right and you, in this scenario, are the customer.'

'It's a shame though. I had just got him how I wanted him. He made the tea just how I like it. Milk to water ratio was spot on. The garden was watered to perfection and he could deadhead like a professional.'

'Shouldn't we chuck something over him? A blanket, perhaps? Just for decency's sake. It feels odd looking at him lying there, that funny colour…'

Stuart disappeared upstairs to get something to cover the body and reappeared with a Peppa Pig duvet in one hand and a file in the other.

'Pulled this off the grandchildren's bed. I didn't fancy using my own duvet. I brought down the paperwork that came with him. Shall we have a cup of tea and a Hobnob and then I can find the number to call. I can't claim my tea is as good as his though.' Stuart gave a little chuckle, looking down at the mound now lying under a smiling Peppa.

'Ah. There is a special number to ring. It says they will, in such circumstances (provided tampering hasn't taken place), deliver a replacement within fourteen working days. They will come and pick up the old one and, provided they still have a DNA sample, set the wheels in motion to grow a new one.'

'That's good, Stu. The old one was, if you don't mind me saying so, looking a little tired. Now you will get a nice new one.'

Stuart walked across the room and lifted the cover. He looked down at his own face staring lifelessly up at him.

'I can see what you mean,' he said, laughing.

Tom Todrum

Sue Duggans

Tom Todrum was a ginger cat,
Handsome, fearless, bright.
He slept by day and fed at dusk
Then prowled around at night.

He lived at number twenty-nine
With kindly Mabel Groat.
She pampered him with tasty treats
And stroked his glossy coat.

When out at night the monstrous tom
Would prowl on padded paw.
With steely eye and pricked-up ear
He'd flex his sharpened claw.

As skies grew black his eyes grew large,
His ears twitched to and fro.
A little mouse or tasty shrew
Would make his juices flow.

Alas, kind Mabel's ginger cat
Loved to spit and fight,
Sometimes during daylight hours
But 'specially at night.

Tom was known as 'King of Cats',
He'd strut with head held high.
His widespread notoriety
Caused other cats to cry!

He'd seek one out, or maybe two,
Then throw the gauntlet down.
With stealth and guile and some brute force
He'd fight to keep his crown.

He'd rip and scratch and bite and snarl,
His emerald eyes would stare.
He'd stop when foe was nearly dead;
He really didn't care!

Tom Todrum then would find a spot
To preen his dusty coat.
He'd lick his paws and wash his face,
Then home to Mabel Groat.

Mrs Groat was quite naïve!
She stroked his shiny fur
And fed him fresh-cooked morsels.
She loved to hear him purr.

One night in early winter
When snow lay thick and chill,
Shameful Tom was ambushed
While strutting up the hill.

At least ten cats came out to fight
From shadowy bush and ditch.
The bullying ginger cat was scared;
It made his whiskers twitch.

They pinned him down with razor claws,
And scratched and bit until
Pain screamed through his furry form,
Then rolled him down the hill.

And finally, when nearly dead,
They left Tom by the wall.
He couldn't move, he wouldn't cry,
He curled up in a ball.

But do not fear, the tale's not done!
He got back on his feet
And limped along to twenty-nine –
Thoughts strayed to Mabel's treat.

He entered through the cat-flap door
Which made a tiny creak.
His mangled, dirty body
Made Mabel squeal and shriek.

It wasn't ripped and tattered ears
Which made poor Mabel wail,
Nor was it bloodied ginger fur
But the really bad twist in the tail!

Love Times Two

Trisha Todd

Still damp with perspiration from their recent exertion, Katrina looked into the bluest pair of eyes she had ever seen and knew without a doubt that this was love. She was hooked, completely, and she realised her life would never be the same again.

Katrina couldn't stop looking at Matthew's face, the line of his nose, his long lashes, that soft mouth that now nuzzled her breast as his naked body curled against hers. She sighed, exhausted, and fulfilled.

'I love you,' she whispered against his blond hair.

It had all started a few months ago and hadn't been planned. Life with her husband, Paul, was settled and Kat was quite happy. He had pulled her pigtails in their primary school assembly, and they had been sweethearts ever since. It was no surprise to their parents and friends that they would marry, and their wedding, four years ago, was the happiest day of Kat's life, at least until now.

Their married life had settled into a comfortable routine. Kat worked in a local accounts office and Paul was an IT manager for the council. They visited friends, hosted dinner parties, went for long, moonlit walks along the beach and

holidayed in hot, foreign lands. They had everything –
nearly, thought Kat. Perhaps life was too settled.

Her love for Matthew had started tentatively at first, and
she hadn't dared hope it would develop further. As the weeks
passed, she found herself sharing her innermost thoughts
with him, her hopes for the future. She knew he was content
to listen to the sound of her voice, confident in her love for
him. Kat sometimes felt guilty about these private times with
him, as she would tell him things, silly things, serious things,
that she couldn't tell Paul.

Things are definitely going to change now, she thought,
and she wondered how Paul would react. Would he take it all
in his stride, as usual, when she explained how she felt?
Would he see she couldn't help loving another, that she had
to be with Matthew – that she loved them both?

She looked across at Paul's tear-stained face and began
to cry as well when he whispered, voice husky with emotion,
'Thank you for our son.'

Margo's Last Journey

Kim Kimber

The train to London is packed. It's exceptionally hot, even for July, perhaps the result of global warming although, according to Giles, the hole in the ozone layer and melting ice caps is all hogwash.

It's still and airless in the carriage, the open windows affording little breeze, as the train crawls along. I feel like a joint of meat in a slow cooker. I am wearing a mask, in spite of restrictions being lifted, making it even more difficult to breathe. Giles is a great believer in conspiracy theories and ridicules my double-jabbed status and devotion to mask-wearing.

'Business can't shut down because a few people have died,' he says. But I continue with my handwashing habits and always wear a face covering in public.

It is also noisy in the train. The school summer holidays having begun, a large proportion of the space is occupied by families. Opposite, a desperate mother bounces a wailing baby against her shoulder, her top absorbing the snot pouring from its nose like green slime. Her two older children are arguing next to her, ignored and unchastised. A large, sweaty man wearing a crumpled suit sits to one side of me, a fidgety youth watching a violent film on his phone to the other. His designer headphones are not sufficiently soundproofed to muffle the heroine's terrified screams.

I put down my Kindle with a sigh, bored with the latest book group saga, and peer outside. My eyes squint against the brightness as we chug through the countryside. Having left the cooling breeze of the estuary behind us, we are travelling slowly through parched fields. Cows shelter from the sweltering heat in patches of shade under the trees and horses swish their tails to bat away flies. A lone cyclist careers along the adjacent path, his progress annoyingly much faster than that of the train. It would be a perfect summer vista if I was not trapped inside a boiling can with Margo.

Owing to the lack of space, my package is stowed on the luggage rack. I have reset the alarm on my phone twice already to remind me that it's there. I was surprised when Giles entrusted me with such an important task but, with him flying into Heathrow from a business trip, I guess he had little choice. Giles travels a lot, brokering big money deals with huge corporations. Even a global pandemic hasn't grounded him for long. I work from my home office, organising fundraising for a charity. Giles's work is high-powered and important, so he says. I guess that means mine is not.

I glance at my watch. I promised that I wouldn't be late. Giles hates my lax time keeping. Realising how important the day is to him, I got up early and chose my outfit with uncharacteristic care. Rejecting my usual uniform of shorts and T-shirt, I am dressed, appropriately I feel, in a plain back linen dress and kitten heels. When I set off, my make-up, for once, looked passable, and my naturally frizzy hair had been tamed into a ponytail, tied with a black ribbon. A nice touch, I thought.

I drain the last of the water from my reusable bamboo flask, wishing I had thought to fill my spare, and take out a compact mirror from my handbag. The face reflected back at me is not the one that left the house an hour and a half earlier. My cheeks are blotchy and red, my skin tacky and both eyes are black rimmed like a panda's. I dab at the damage with a tissue but that just seems to make it worse. Giles admires girls who have eyeliner and lip gloss permanently etched on their faces, the kind whose images stare out vacantly from ads on billboards and in glossy magazines. This is not me!

The train shivers to a halt and the perspiring passengers let out a collective groan.

Apologetic messages from the rail company have punctuated the journey. We mortals are not the only thing suffering in the heatwave, apparently. The rails are too hot and in danger of buckling, causing the train to slow down. And now stop. The driver's voice assures everyone that the train will be moving again soon. At least Giles's mother, Margo, tucked away in the luggage rack, can't blame me for the delay.

When she found out that she was dying, Margo had made her wishes very clear. Born and brought up in London, it was no surprise that she wanted the capital to be her final resting place, but her request that her ashes be scattered on the River

Thames came as bit of a shock. Giles nearly spat out his expensive macchiato, made from the finest hand-ground beans, when she told him. Let's just say he would prefer a more permanent, solid reminder, like the imposing Victorian grave architecture in Highgate Cemetery that he so admires. But even Giles wouldn't go against his mother, dead or alive.

Margo had transformed herself via a series of prosperous marriages, the second of which produced Giles, during a time when women had fewer options to be independent. I think it a fitting end; the river's journey through the various boroughs and hamlets, affluent and poor, reflecting the two stages of her life, from Madge to Margo.

The train stop-starts into the next station on the outskirts of the furnace that is London and even more people attempt to squeeze into the already packed carriage. I can bear it no longer. I carefully retrieve what remains of Margo, the biodegradable urn disguised in a Harrods shopper, and emerge like a moth from a cocoon onto the platform. I pull down my mask and breathe in a lungful of warm air before walking across to the underground, Margo swinging gently by my side.

The Tube is surprisingly quiet after the busy overland train but no less hot. I collapse gratefully into a seat, placing the bag on the one beside me, thankful for the lack of commuters at this time on a Friday. I pull out my phone before we descend into the tunnel but there is no spark of life, although I swear that I put it on to charge last night. Then I remember pulling out the cable to plug in my laptop so that I could check train times. I now have no way of contacting Giles. I imagine him rushing out of the airport and jumping into a cab, grinding his teeth when he can't reach me.

The underground train progresses slowly but at least keeps moving. Numerous stations remain between me and my destination, Westminster, where I am due to meet Giles for the short walk to Lambeth Pier. I ponder his dilemma if I don't arrive on time. He can hardly hold the ceremony without me, seeing as I have his mother's ashes in my possession. We'll have to rebook for another day, meaning further expense and rearranging of his busy schedule. And a lot more teeth grinding, no doubt.

At the next stop, a group of women, each wearing bunny ears, pour into the carriage, whooping and giggling. A hen party. They dance about, reckless and maskless, passing round an open bottle of prosecco and singing 'I Will Survive' loudly and out of tune. The hens are dressed in pink frothy tutus while the bride, in a tight, white corset, has a large 'L' plate pinned to her butt. I move further down the carriage, wondering what it would be like to plan a wedding. Giles doesn't believe in marriage, the result of one too many stepfathers, each entering his life for a short time only to leave again. But I am more traditional and see it as a public declaration of our love for one another.

Around half an hour later, the train stops at Tower Hill and the passengers are forced to alight. The drunken hens lurch, as one, towards the electronic doors. Clutching the Harrods shopper tightly, I step onto the packed platform. My dress is sticking uncomfortably to my back and my new shoes are rubbing painfully on my heels. Giles had been so pleased that the forecast was good for his mother's final, important day but who could have predicted an unprecedented heatwave? I hate the heat. Margo knew that so maybe this is her final revenge on a girlfriend who was never quite good enough for her only son.

A glance at the station clock confirms the terrible truth; not only am I late but, unless I can get to Westminster in two minutes, we risk losing our slot on *The Guvnor*. I consider taking my chances above ground and calling an Uber but remember my phone is currently useless. Giles, of course, never leaves home without a portable charger and power pack.

Eventually, a Circle Line train comes into view. It glides slowly into the station, oblivious of the need for urgency, and I wait impatiently for the doors to open. At least everyone appears to be adhering to the underground mask policy. Inside the carriage, the herd keep one another upright. There is nothing to hold on to so I stand and sway to the train's rhythm with Margo, happily free from the risk of Covid, squashed against my leg.

Nothing is visible through the knot of passengers so I listen carefully as each station is announced. People sweat and sigh as the train progresses slowly through baking tunnels. Finally, we reach Westminster and I escape gratefully from the confines of the carriage. I stand and watch as the train departs, rummaging in my handbag for my ticket. Then I realise. Margo is no longer with me.

Light-headedness overcomes me that could be due to the

heat, exhaustion or dehydration. More likely, it is the thought of Giles's reaction when I tell him that I have left his mother on the Tube. He will call me irresponsible and stupid and uncaring. Maybe I am but, strangely, I find that I no longer care what Giles thinks. And, in a way, I have fulfilled Margo's dying wish; her remains are currently circling London, just not exactly in the way she anticipated.

Smiling broadly, I cross the platform and board a train in the opposite direction.

Best Served Cold

Pat Sibbons

Doreen was sure they were talking about her. The minute they saw her coming up the aisle they stopped their conversation abruptly and looked down at their lisianthus.

'Morning, Doreen,' said Eileen cheerily. 'And what a beautiful morning it is too.'

'Isn't it,' replied Doreen, tight lipped. She took her seat at the table with the rest of the group preparing the church flowers.

She knew it wasn't her imagination. Eileen and Judith kept exchanging knowing looks. The three had been friends for years and, apart from 'The Thursford Incident' of 1998, had always got along marvellously.

They were a bit off with me last week too, she thought. They had met at Judith's on Friday. Each week they took turns to host the others for coffee and cake and, once a month, they went out to dinner at the Badger and Duck. She had mentioned the new Italian restaurant in town to them. Her cousin had been there and said it was amazing. Fabulous authentic Italian food, superb wines and attentive service.

'Do you fancy trying Il Carlotta for our next meal out?'

she had asked them.

'Oh no,' said Eileen pulling a sour face. 'I've heard it's very expensive. And dreadfully noisy. The pub is much better value.'

Doreen was so disappointed. Eileen was usually very easy going and almost annoyingly positive about everything, a fun person to be around despite her strange habit of clicking her teeth when she concentrated. The preparation of the Christmas flowers last year had been hugely challenging! The click, click, click had nearly driven her mad.

'I was just thinking, with it being my birthday soon, it would be nice to go somewhere different.'

'But just say it's not very good?' said Judith. 'You will be so disappointed. I think it's best if we stick to the pub. We know what we are getting at the Badger and Duck.'

We certainly do, thought Doreen. *Boring old sausage and mash or scampi and chips. And the barman! He always has a sweaty forehead! When did they turn into such mean, boring old ladies? Their dead husbands have seen they aren't short of a few bob!*

When all the flowers had been sufficiently arranged, Doreen repacked her scissors and twine in her RHS tote. 'I'll see you both at my house tomorrow for coffee then,' she said as she turned on her heels and marched back up the aisle. She was very upset. Her friends had barely spoken to her all morning. They had kept their heads down and she was sure they were whispering behind that enormous bunch of gyp.

She needed cheering up and so caught the number 96 into town. A trip to the library and Boots usually helped her to feel better.

As she walked back to the stop to catch the bus home, she saw two familiar figures emerging from Il Carlotta. Arm in arm and looking thoroughly smug, Judith and Eileen chirped their way up the street, totally unaware of poor, distressed Doreen peering out from behind the bus shelter.

***

'Come in. Judith is here already.' A smiling Eileen followed Doreen up the hall to the living room. 'Make yourselves at home while I make the coffee.'

Doreen quietly closed the kitchen door behind her. She was so enraged by her friends' deceit she felt almost anaesthetised. The kettle had boiled, a spoonful of coffee was in each mug, the milk was out of the fridge and the sugar bowl was on standby. She would teach them to ostracise her. How dare they treat her like this? She opened her handbag and took out her eye drops. She was tempted to put a few drops in her eyes, as they were very dry. She thought perhaps dry eyes were a symptom of rage. After all, she had never been this angry in her entire life. Not even in the aftermath of 'Thursford'. Carefully, she squeezed the eye drops into the pink peonies (for Judith) and the other half into yellow roses (for Eileen). A splash of milk in each and she was ready to serve her 'friends' their coffee. She hoped the terrible stomach cramps and appalling diarrhoea wouldn't last more than a couple of days.

She was already feeling better as she handed her friends

their drinks. Now they were about to pay for their crimes, she was able to enjoy the conversation about the organist's latest faux pas without feeling resentful. As they neared the bottom of their mugs she was feeling smug. When the last drop of coffee was drained a feeling of peace descended over her.

Eileen put her mug back on the tray, took a fondant fancy and turned towards Doreen, who said, 'We have a surprise for you. We want to do something special for your birthday. You have been such a good friend to us over the years and we want to show you how much we care, so we have booked a table at that new Italian place you mentioned. We booked it a week ago but popped into town yesterday to see the manager and make sure everything is going to be perfect. It is so stylish and the food looks delicious. Much more exciting than the pub!'

'The table is reserved from seven-thirty this evening,' said Judith. 'There's a cab picking you up at seven. We're having champagne, balloons, the works. All you need to do is put on your face and glad rags.'

Doreen stared at her friends in horrified silence.

'Well, say something,' said Eileen.

'I feel funny,' said Judith.

Lucille's Doll

Barbara Sleap

It was Friday at last and Kate switched off her laptop. She was halfway through writing her second novel *Lives and Times* which she was finding much harder than the first. That's why she was staying at the eighteenth-century Chantry Grange Hotel. She'd secured a good rate for room 125 at the quiet side of the building. Here she had no distractions, no telephone calls, no deliveries to take in for her neighbours (who must be Amazon's best customers) and no noise from the block of flats being hastily erected in the next road. She stayed here during the week and returned home to spend the weekends with her ever-patient husband, Jerry. Her publisher had given her until May to finish the first draft and it was now March. Time was marching on.

There was only one drawback to room 125; several times during her stay she had been woken in the night by the image of a young girl dressed in long, white nightwear. Initially, Kate thought she was dreaming. The girl, who was aged about ten, had dark, curled hair partially covered by a frilly nightcap. She was cuddling a small doll dressed in similar night attire. Surprisingly, Kate hadn't felt afraid, as a strange calm had spread through the room. The child said, in a soft voice, 'Mama, help me, Mama,' and had stood for a minute or two before fading away.

Chantry Grange was set amid large parklands with a walled garden abundant with colour even at this time of year. It was now midday and Kate needed to stretch her legs and get some fresh air. This had become her usual routine; a walk followed by sandwiches and coffee in the hotel's Sun Lounge Café. Sometimes, she ate dinner there too but most often she drove to a popular little Italian in the nearby village of Chantry Wood.

Kate walked out towards the end of the walled garden where work was in progress building an orangery. She was told it was to be an alternative wedding and events venue. Kate stood behind the yellow tape and watched the workmen laying foundations or clearing earth thrown up by the excavator. She had got to know a couple of them and received friendly waves as she watched them work.

Just then, a loud whistle blew and the men stopped as the foreman held up his hand. Several of the men peered down into an exposed trench. A lot of shouting and scurrying ensued. Kate was curious and walked around the taped off area. Tom, one of the men she knew, sauntered towards her.

'What's happened, Tom?'

'Worst thing that could happen on a building site; we've unearthed a body. Well, not really a body, just a skeleton. It'll stop work for some time I can tell you. Boss won't be too pleased. It will put the schedule back and cost money.'

Kate stayed for a while as a small crowd of guests and hotel staff watched police cars and a team of forensic officers arrive to investigate. Eventually, they were all told to leave by the stressed hotel manager. Kate returned to her room and tried to concentrate on *Lives and Times*.

Despite her enquiries, no information about the skeleton was forthcoming until the end of the following week. Kate was eager for news of the discovery and asked again at the reception desk. A man standing nearby, who had obviously heard her question, turned towards Kate.

'Hello! I heard you asking about the discovery the other Friday. Do you work here?'

Kate shook her head and explained that she was a regular guest.

'Do they know who it is yet?' she enquired.

'Oh yes, an old family mystery has been solved. The police have ascertained it is the remains of little Lucille Denton who used to live here with her family. Apparently, she disappeared when she was just ten years old.'

Kate swallowed and held onto the desk.

'Ten years old,' she stuttered.

The man saw her distress and led her to a nearby chair.

He introduced himself. 'I'm Guy Denton. My family have owned this house since 1790 and my ancestors have lived here ever since. The story of the missing child has been passed down through the generations.

'Her parents, Jane and Max Denton, had three children. Lucille was the youngest and, rumour has it, she was a very difficult child. Her mother and a succession of nannies and governesses were unable to deal with her violent tantrums and strange behaviour. I suppose in today's world she would be classed as autistic. Lucille disappeared amid much secrecy and speculation; tales of her living with distant relatives, being sent to boarding school or that she had simply run away. It caused gossip in the village for years. The mystery of what happened to her remained unsolved – until now.'

Kate felt a shiver run through her body.

'Are they sure it's her?' she asked.

'As certain as can be. It wasn't just her bones they found, there was something strange as well. Found amongst the remains was the small doll that Lucille always carried. According to notes written and left by one of the governesses, Lucille always dressed the doll, which she had named Lulu, in the same clothes as herself. Apparently, it was one of her many obsessions.'

Guy touched Kate's arm. 'Hey, are you okay? You've gone very pale.'

Kate jumped slightly and nodded.

Guy continued. 'It's really spooky, the doll was completely intact even down to the tiny yellow dress. it looked as if Lucille had been buried holding it in her arms.'

Kate attended the sad little funeral held for Lucille at the village chapel. Guy was there with his family, members of the hotel staff, and Tom with his boss. Within the small white coffin Lucille's bones had been covered by a pretty yellow dress, expertly copied from the doll's by a local seamstress. Lulu had been ceremoniously placed next to the remains.

Kate watched as the coffin was lowered into a grave near

to Lucille's parents and siblings where she belonged. The mystery of how she had died remained unsolved.

Kate never saw her night-time visitor again. When she returned home, she showed Jerry the story in the local paper but kept the visitations to herself, her secret. She finished *Lives and Times* by the due date. On the fly leaf she commemorated it to:

Lucille Denton and Lulu of Chantry Grange
Rest in Peace

The Last Dance

Kim Kimber

The road to Tyburn is packed, the route lined by people of all ages. Our carriage moves slowly through the crowds passing yeomen, farmers, poor wretches in rags and apprentices happy to have been given the day off. There is only one man who will swing today but, still, there can be few workers left in England; they are all making their way here. A hanging is a public event, seen by many as fine sport, but I have no desire to witness another lose his life, particularly a gentle man with whom I have danced in the moonlight.

'You look pale, my dear,' the voice of my husband, William, interrupts my thoughts. 'Are you well? You have hardly spoken since we left home.'

'I am quite well, thank you.'

'But you are shivering,' he says, pulling the blanket further around me. 'Best take care, my love. We don't want you catching a chill.' He takes my hand in his sweaty palm and I recoil slightly. My husband's face is red and bloated under his periwig and hat, in spite of the cold, and his plump lips have formed into a smug smile.

'It is merely the January air,' I say dismissively.

William waves to passers-by as the carriage bumps and shakes towards the gallows. 'Not long now, my dear,' he says, 'and we shall see that rascal get what he deserves.'

I nod and pull the hood of my cloak further over my face so that he cannot read my expression. Unlike my husband, I do not wish to see this highwayman hanged. He may have robbed from those who have more than enough to give but he has never harmed another and I cannot bear the thought of his life being cut short by the hangman's noose.

At last the uncomfortable journey ends and my husband helps me down from the carriage. 'Come along, my dear,' he says cheerfully, 'we want to be sure of the best view.'

William leads me through the crowd to a row of rough, wooden seats, on a raised platform, specially erected for the occasion. We are positioned in clear sight of the gallows, flanked on all sides by lords, ladies and gentlemen, and those passing beneath us nod and doff their caps. The death bells can be heard ringing faintly in the distance marking the slow progress of the procession from Newgate to Tyburn, stopping at church and tavern to satisfy man's last earthly needs.

A boy walks past banging a riddle drum and with each beat the cart bearing the accused to his death rattles nearer. I turn away from my husband so he will not see my tears. He cannot know the highwayman stole more than worldly riches on that cloudless night when he held up our coach.

His name is a whisper, like a kiss on my lips; Claude Du Vall. I remember well his wild, dark hair, flamboyant attire, gallant nature and those twinkling eyes that shone through the holes in his black mask like bright stars. He of whom I should have been afraid certainly made my heart beat faster, but not from fear. His gentle manners and soft accent posed little threat and the memory of that moonlit night, when we danced the courante under a cloudless sky, still burns brightly.

***

We were returning home, travelling across Hounslow Heath. The hour was late and darkness surrounded the coach when the highwayman made his move. We heard a shout and we were propelled forward inside the carriage as the horses were brought to an abrupt halt by the man William later described as 'a pistol waving devil'. The door of the coach was pulled open to reveal our assailant and the moment I saw him, I knew it was Du Vall. News of the Frenchman had travelled far.

Not knowing what to do, I took out my flageolet and began to play a merry tune.

'Put that away,' said William, 'it may anger the rascal. Do you want to get us all killed?'

'We are in no danger,' I replied. 'The Monsieur is after our money, not our lives,' but I obeyed my husband and immediately put down the recorder. To our company's surprise, and the merriment of Du Vall's accomplices who had by now surrounded the coach, the melody continued. The highwayman had begun to play a flageolet of his own and bade me to join in with him. William's cheeks turned a deep puce as the sound of music filled the Heath.

***

It is approaching noon as the procession comes into view. The cart bearing the condemned man, and those who will see him off, is surrounded by cavalry. Claude is sat atop the wooden box that will inter his remains, pinioned between hangman and priest, devil and God's appointed. He is dressed like a gentleman in a blood red, embroidered jacket, silk waistcoat and black breeches. Even from a distance I can see that the rumours are true. Unmasked, he is indeed handsome with delicate, fine features.

I breathe in sharply and William pats my hand. 'There, my dear,' he says. 'Calm yourself. It will soon be over and that dreadful night will be nought but a bad dream. You will quickly forget.' But I don't want to. I will remember, always…

***

When we had stopped playing our instruments, Du Vall turned to my husband and demanded to see the contents of his purse. William's hands shook as he undid the clasp to reveal four hundred pounds.

'I will not take all of your money, sir,' said the highwayman, 'if your lady will do me the honour of joining me in a dance.' He turned his head slightly to wink at me.

Without looking to me for my consent, William nodded, too intent on preserving his fortune to concern himself about besmirching my reputation.

Monsieur Du Vall took my hand and helped me down from the coach. He gestured to our companions to strike up a tune and we began to move in time to the music. My limbs were stiff from travelling but we quickly found our rhythm and I danced as with no other before him. Claude could well have been mistaken for a gentleman in his fancy breeches and French riding boots, his movements practised and fluid. Indeed, I found it liberating to dance with someone who was not hindered by age and the effects of too much liquor. It seemed that Monsieur Du Vall had bewitched the whole company, for they quickly gathered round clapping and cheering, with the exception of William who was too cowardly to move from the coach.

Du Vall was true to his word and returned the sum of one hundred pounds to my husband.

***

The sounds and sights of that night fade and are replaced by others as the cart approaches the gallows. People in the assembled crowd jeer and shout as the other occupants of the cart jump down leaving Du Vall alone to face his end. For him there will be no earthly pardon as there was too little time between sentencing and punishment to make entreaties to the king. I suspect William's hand in deciding the highwayman's fate, as the judge is a close friend of his.

If Claude is afraid, he does not show it. He waves theatrically to the crowd, smiling and blowing kisses to the circle of weeping women who have pushed forward to grieve at his feet. I am allowed no such luxury.

The priest, Bible in hand, raises his arm and the crowd falls silent, eager to hear the highwayman's last words. 'There is much to regret in this life,' he says, his accent more pronounced than I remember. 'I have done more than most to need God's pardon but there are some deeds for which I make no apology...'

At this, the women surrounding the cart begin to weep louder, their hands outstretched in an attempt to touch the highwayman's feet, whether for luck or in memory of carnal pleasure I know not, but Claude pays them no attention. Instead, those dark eyes search the masses until his gaze meets mine.

I feel William's grip around my arm like a snare as Du Vall continues. 'There is one night, above all others, that has made this life worth the trouble and for that I am grateful. I would gladly return all the riches I have taken in return for one last dance.'

William splutters at my side. 'Enough of this nonsense,' he shouts. 'Hang the brigand, 'tis time he danced the Tyburn jig.'

Some of the crowd whoop and holler as the heavy noose is placed around Claude's neck. I sway unsteadily on the bench but am held in place by William and the surrounding mob. Our connection does not break as the hangman places a hood over the highwayman's head and the horses attached to the cart are slapped away. Only then do I close my eyes.

Claude's last moments are measured out by the baying crowd, like a drove of angry donkeys, but he does not hear them above the flageolet's delicate tune. He is no longer twisting on the gallows but on Hounslow Heath, with a beautiful girl on his arm, dancing the courante.

Claude Du Vall was a French-born highwayman who was hanged at Tyburn in 1670. Allegedly, he never harmed those he robbed and had a reputation for being a womaniser. This famous story of how Du Vall, having held up a coach on Hounslow Heath, requested a dance with the lady within in exchange for not taking all of the gentleman's money has been passed down through the centuries.

Polly and Rod

Sue Duggans

The body lay crumpled and still. A fatal blow had seen to that. Wide-open eyes glistened slightly and didn't seem as lifeless as the corpse. Teeth were visible.

Looking down at the dead body, Polina, known as Polly, shuddered. She felt an equal measure of guilt and relief that this intrusion in her life was over. Since the day that Rod had moved in she'd lived in fear of him and her heart beat faster every time their eyes met. She didn't even know if Rod was actually his name. What a mess!

Until today, thoughts of Rod invaded the quiet spaces of her mind throughout the day and his presence in Polly's life had become very testing. Some time ago, he'd tiptoed in without a sound while she was mopping the kitchen floor and, oblivious of her unease, crept right up in front of her staring all the while, scrutinising. Polly had jumped out of her skin and let out a loud, piercing scream. She'd tried to hit Rod with the mop but he had ducked out of her way.

Recently, he'd stayed away for several days and Polly had no idea where he'd gone. She knew that Rod had enemies and wondered if he'd been attacked but a couple of evenings ago, as she was watching TV, he walked in as bold as anything and looked her in the eye.

'Don't you go bringing any of your filthy friends back here,' she'd said to him. He'd tilted his head slightly to one side, which she'd seen him do before, but didn't respond.

'Having you here for this long is beyond a joke but friends, no way!'

Before anything more could be said, he'd hurried silently into the kitchen.

'Don't leave a mess in there,' she'd called after him and, with a touch of agitated shrillness in her voice, added, 'I'm fed up with clearing up after you!'

Quiet!

Later that night, just as Polly was falling into a fitful sleep, she'd felt him stroke against her face. She had sat bolt upright and screamed, 'Don't come near me! You beast! You've done enough harm.'

She could smell him in the pitch dark room but, startled by her outburst, he'd kept his distance. It was then, in the dead of night and with sleep eluding her, that Polly had hatched her plan.

This can't go on, she'd thought to herself, her eyes tightly closed and her breathing shallow. *He won't leave of his own accord so I'll have to do something drastic.*

Polly returned from work the next day armed with all she required and prepared herself with unease and trepidation for the final blow. She poured herself a glass of whisky and took two large gulps. The snap as the metal bar hit his neck filled her with horror! She watched as a small amount of bright red blood dribbled from his ear. She covered the lifeless form and curled up on the sofa, numbed by her second, large glass of whisky.

'That's that over!' she mumbled.

Pulling a fleece up tight around her to protect from the chill and stop the shivering, she slurred out loud, 'I'll deal with you in the morning.' Then she fell into anaesthetised sleep.

The next morning, despite the whisky, Polly felt strangely revitalised. She bounced into the kitchen and put the kettle on. She opened the blind and squinted as bright sunshine streamed in. As she pulled on her Marigolds she sang lines from Elton John's well-known track: 'I'm Still Standing'.

Taking a clean food container from the bottom drawer she went to where the covered corpse lay. In one swift move she whipped off the cover, lifted the trap and noiselessly dropped the stiff little rodent into the container.

The Anecdote

Pat Sibbons

I look across the table at Pete with contempt. Hadn't I asked him to avoid telling silly stories tonight? Hadn't he agreed not to avail our friends of his ridiculous tales? It is like an illness, I think. He just can't help it. I had asked him, really nicely. I hadn't been angry or nasty. I had simply asked him that, for once, he not make up some stupid rubbish.

Karen has got 'Delia' out and gone to a lot of trouble. It is Tom's 60th and the wine is flowing but Pete is in the centre of things again, talking utter drivel.

I think I'm a fairly patient individual. I rub along with most people. But Pete… He has many good qualities. He is kind, loyal and generous. At home he has developed some strange habits as he has got older; moving things and making funny noises amongst them. I can cope when we are on our own but I can't stand it when he tries to take centre stage amongst our friends. It has taken me months to get over the story he told at the pub quiz. The one about the woman who was breastfeeding in the park when a seagull swooped down and carried off the baby before dropping it in the boating lake. He insisted it was true. It happened during the war. His mother had witnessed it. As she is long dead I can't confirm the truth of the matter. I know a lot of weird stuff happened during the war, but really?

And now, here he is, with five pairs of eyes and five pairs of ears, all focussed on him.

'So, apparently, this woman was doing the ironing in the kitchen of her home in Camden when the doorbell rings. She opens it and guess who is standing there?'

'Idi Amin?' says Roy with a smirk. He's on to him, I think. He knows Pete is going to make a complete prat of himself again.

'No,' says Pete grinning, 'but good effort. Anyone else?'

'Fred Scuttle?' says Tom with a straight face. But in his eyes he is definitely laughing.

'No,' says Pete. 'You know very well that Fred Scuttle is a Benny Hill character. He is, therefore, unlikely to be ringing doorbells in Camden!'

'Any more Merlot?' enquires Karen, clearly trying to diffuse the ticking bomb that is one of Pete's stories.

'Ann Widdecombe?' says Janet.

'I can't stand that bloody woman,' Karen interjects. 'Just because she allowed herself to be hauled around a dance floor like a sack of spuds, she thinks she is a celebrity!'

'Isn't he gay?' says Janet looking perplexed.

'Who? Fred Scuttle?' laughs Roy.

'No, not Fred Scuttle, Anton.'

'No. He's married with twins. To a woman!'

'Well, he wouldn't be the first gay man to be married to a woman and have children.'

'Okay. As interesting as all this is, you are not even warm. Standing on her doorstep was Bob Dylan.'

Everyone looks a bit unimpressed. Karen is topping up the glasses, probably hoping everyone will pass out before the punchline. Pete ploughs on.

'So here he is, Bob Dylan, standing on her doorstep. "Hi, ma'am," says Bob. "Is Dave at home?"'

'It turns out the woman's husband, Dave, is having the car serviced. She doesn't recognise Bob so just assumes he is one of her other half's mates. She asks him in for a cup of tea while he waits. They have a lovely chat about the weather, cats, all sorts. She even got out her gingernuts for him. Properly put the world to rights they did. About forty-five minutes later, Dave gets home. He immediately recognises Mr Dylan and nearly has a coronary as he sees him sitting at his breakfast bar watching his wife ironing the bedlinen. Apparently, the world-famous music producer and ex-Eurythmic, Dave Stewart, lived in the same road and Bob Dylan had just knocked on the wrong door.'

'Bullshit!' shouts Tom, spurred on by the Sainsbury's finest Pinot Grigio. 'Really, Pete. You have come out with some crap before but this is absolute tommyrot! Firstly, who wouldn't recognise Bob Dylan. Secondly, what are the chances of him knocking on the wrong door and it happens to belong to someone called Dave?'

'Brandy anyone? Baileys, Tia Maria, Disaronno?' As the liqueurs are passed around, Roy continues the attack.

'What was Bob Dylan doing in Camden, wandering about without an entourage?'

'I can only assume he was hoping to discuss a future or current project with Mr Stewart. As for being alone, he may be a world-famous recording artist but he isn't exactly Donald Trump!'

'Don't mention that Cheeto-eating, shit-gibbon,' says a giggling Janet.

'Well, I think that is a lovely story, Pete. More brandy anyone?' Karen really is the Henry Kissinger of every dinner party.

'Exactly!' shouts a slurring Tom. 'Exactly! A story, Pete, mate. You're a nice guy but this is just made up shite. Can't we talk about normal stuff for once? Football, what's on the telly. Anything other than the tripe you spout.'

'It is absolutely true! I heard Bob Dylan talking about it during a radio interview and the Camden woman actually rang in to confirm it.'

Roy sniggered and said, 'What was the date you heard the programme. Beginning of April was it?'

Everyone is now howling with laughter. Apart from me.

'No, it bloody wasn't! It was back in June, I think. I remember I was listening to the radio in the garage while getting the car ready for the Dawlish trip.'

It is either the wine talking or the mention of Dawlish but now they are wetting themselves.

'Right. That's it. Come on, we are leaving.'

I drain my glass and look over at Karen who, to be fair, doesn't look at all bothered by our imminent departure.

Pete has stropped off into the hall to get our coats as I go around the table saying goodbye and apologising.

'Not your fault. We are used to Pete's thrilling anecdotes but I think tonight's just sent us over the edge.'

Pete hands me my coat as he exits the front door. Clearly it will be some time before he is over tonight's humiliation. Maybe, if we are lucky, it will curb his anecdotes altogether.

I do hope so. The thing is, I was listening to that same radio programme in the kitchen that day. Who knew Bob Dylan likes gingernuts?

Utopia

Lois Maulkin

Aah, my chair, my chair, I remember. That one I painted, it was here once, among the coffee smell and the thick vanillaryness.

We're having toast. And Marmite. And tea. And here's a sponge-soft sofa made Battenburg by the blanket on its back. Not known you long, have I? A couple of weeks, jokes on WhatsApp, considered replies trying to sound off the cuff. We are less polished now than when we met last night. Far too much of the red, I'm afraid. I like you. You calm my pulse.

I watch you pouring sugar from a sachet. Why is it funny? Something about the angle of your fingers. Here's my tea. Ha! Slopped in the saucer. You offer the toast plate. We talk as we eat; you choke on crumbs, I laugh. You pretend offence and splutter. I like you more.

There are pictures on the walls. This is a place for art and artists. The jam lines of sustaining cake grin out through glass domes and big silver machines make the perfect cup of whatever. You don't know about my chair.

Last night's wine makes me rheumy and bleurgh. You too, you say, butter in your beard. A man in a wing chair, under a sundae painting of somewhere local but squished, is on the phone.

'Catheters,' he's shouting, 'then the complete evisceration of my stomach lining.'

Simultaneous putting down of toast. You and I look sideways at each other. Sniggering together, children sharing nursery tea.

My systems calm. Things seem set fair. The town outside is cold and grey as the estuary but we are warm and wrapped in the steam of hot drinks. Granny-square crochet, massed regiments of fruit tarts, nestles us. Your eyes are dark and soft. Dabs of treacle. Not searing or spells, I think. Not dragons. But something.

A tiny boat sails across the circular sea of my tea, and rests at the far side of the cup. I bend to look, so close my hair ends get wet.

You and I sit inside, eating toast and Marmite, laughing. Utopia!

The Magical Garden

Michele Hawkins

Tonight we are going to visit a magical walled garden, many centuries old. We approach the garden by tiptoeing through soft strands of grass swaying in the gentle breeze. As we take a deep breath, the scent of wild meadow flowers is intoxicating. Balmy blue and lilac mix harmoniously with bright red, yellow and orange. Stooping down for a closer look, we gently brush against the delicate petals. All around us dandelions are dancing prettily in the teasing light wind, giving up their seeds to the cloudless sky.

Presently we come across a rustic, red brick wall. On closer inspection we see that the bricks are in fact many different shades of red. Some are a chalky white in places, cooked by the sun over many, many years. The nooks and crannies are a playground for small insects, providing shade and shelter.

We walk in the long grass by the wall, trailing our fingertips lazily along the brick, acknowledging the contrasting roughness and smoothness. The bricks still retain some warmth from the heat of the day that is ending now. We reach an old wooden door, ajar. Stretching out, we push it with both hands, feeling the grooves in the greying wood, weathered and silky from years of guarding the garden. It swings open on oiled hinges without noise or protest to display a beautiful garden, guarded by the tall, red wall. Strong, safe, secure.

Stepping into the garden we take another deep, relaxing inhalation, breathing in the enticing, evocative scent of exotic flowers before slowly releasing our breath. Looking around, we spot the place where the gorgeous perfume originates. Hundreds of big, bold, blousy blooms, fascinating shapes, a kaleidoscope of colour, beckon to us to investigate. Heading over, we admire the diversity, stroking the showy canopy of tropical leaves that cast a long shadow over the flowers and the grass we are standing on. Spreading out ahead of us, under an archway of sweet-smelling purple clematis and pink roses twined together in friendship and peace, is a moss-covered path leading to a fountain.

Walking slowly forward, our bare feet sink blissfully into the carpet of spongy, damp moss. As we get closer to the fountain, we see that it is a sculpture of an angel. Her harp is playing the music of the water, tinkling into the bowl of the fountain ready to be played again, over and over. Calming tunes, soothing to the soul. Cupping our hands together, we capture some of the cool, sparkling water. We drink deeply, enjoying the sensation of the nectar slipping down our throats, quenching our thirst.

To our left is another path, this one is made from slabs of smooth limestone. As we wander along listening closely, we can hear insects buzzing and birds chirping, saying goodnight to each other, and then a hushed silence surrounds us in tranquillity. As dusk draws over us gradually, we see a tiny light, flickering in front of a hollow in the trunk of an old oak tree. As we watch, it is joined by another and another until our path is helpfully illuminated by fireflies.

Coming to the end of the path we hear a gently babbling brook, the water dancing over slippery stones and making the occasional splash. Walking beside the brook we glimpse the shimmering silver of small fish frolicking on their journey downstream. The tendrils of weeping willows tickle our faces and the clean, crisp smell of clear water is in our nostrils as we come to a lake.

The lake is fringed with bulrushes, whispering secrets to each other as they nod in the gentle breeze. It is subtly lit by the moonlight casting a silver, glittering glimmer that stretches across to the opposite bank, delicately illuminating the gracious, gliding swans which barely disturb the water as they drift, their elegant long necks lying over their wings, tucking themselves in for the night.

Moving more ponderously now, overcome with tiredness, our legs feel heavy, feet start to drag, we spy a boat tethered to a post just ahead. Upon reaching it we carefully climb in. Untying the rope and pushing away from the post, we float slowly off towards the middle of the lake. The floor of the boat is covered in invitingly thick throws. Yawning widely and with heavy eyes we snuggle into the comfortable cosiness of the throws. Covering our bodies with one, we are totally cocooned in warmth and peace. The boat is gently rocking, the water caressing it as we are enveloped in a loving cuddle and lulled off to a deep, restful, restorative sleep.

About the Authors

Sue Duggans

Sue's previous passion for writing was reignited after joining the writing group several years ago. The monthly meetings provide her with an opportunity to share and discuss work as well as enjoy the company of established friends.

Sue enjoys knitting and sewing, travelling in the UK, walking and birdwatching which is a relatively new hobby. She is a proud and privileged mum and granny.

Michele Hawkins

Michele fell in love with books at a young age. An avid reader, she has an eclectic taste covering many genres. Having joined this friendly, supportive bunch a few years ago, this is the second anthology she has contributed to.

Michele works part time which allows her to pursue a few hobbies including Pilates, walking, singing in a fun choir and, most recently, joining her local branch of The Bluetits Chill Swimmers. She has every intention of swimming in the sea throughout winter. We'll see!

Kim Kimber

Reading and writing have always featured in Kim's life. She devoured books from a young age and later wrote short stories and articles for magazines, going on to become editor of a local parenting magazine. Kim loves her current role as a freelance book editor, helping authors on their journey to publication.

She co-founded Light Bulb Quizzes in 2015 and compiles quiz questions for books and games. Prior to the pandemic, she had a fabulous time at conventions (showcasing TV shows, films, and all things related to pop culture) selling books, talking to fans and meeting actors. Her favourite to date remains Jeffrey Dean Morgan.

Kim is married with three grown-up children. She enjoys Pilates and swimming and has recently started the huge task of tracing her family tree. She lives close to the seafront where she walks every day.

Lois Maulkin

Lois has written regular columns for an assortment of magazines and organisations local to her hometown of Southend-on-Sea. By day she manages a charity shop, in the evenings she likes to read, write and paint, though not at the same time!

A mum of four, and guardian of a cat that registers fairly high up on the snooty scale, she has recently given up mowing the lawn and now dwells in a small damp house in the tiniest meadow in Essex.

Pat Sibbons

Pat is the newest member of the group. Originally from London, she has lived in Leigh-on-Sea with her family for nearly thirty years.

Working part time as a sessional worker for a young carers' charity and as a dog walker keep her busy. Yoga keeps her active. She loves writing and has tinkered in the past, but being a member of Phoenix has become a passion of hers. She loves the creativity, the laughs and being part of such a warm and caring group of women.

Barbara Sleap

At seventy-five, Barbara is the oldest member of the group. She has two sons and five grandchildren who keep her active and young at heart, and is a keen member of the aqua aerobics classes at her gym.

She has a passion for historic buildings and, as a retired travel consultant, has explored some of the best. Nowadays she likes nothing better than a summer picnic in the grounds of a castle or stately home with like-minded friends.

Being an avid reader, she has always had an interest in the written word and takes great pleasure in completing the challenging tasks set by Kim. Barbara is proud to belong to Phoenix Writing Group because, through their writing, the members have become firm friends.

Trisha Todd

Trisha has decorated, moved, renovated, decorated again, recovered from illness and an operation and gained more grandchildren, which is why there are not many of her stories within these pages. She really hopes you like them though.

Hopefully, normal service will be resumed soon.

About Southend in Sight

Southend in Sight is the Community Services Division of Southend Blind Welfare Organisation (Registered Charity no. 1069765) and has provided help and support for local people experiencing visual impairment since it was set up in 1958.

It is an independent charity and at its headquarters in Hamlet Court Road, VIPs (Visually Impaired Persons) can find out about, and try out, specialist equipment for the home before hiring or buying, as well as learn about help and benefits available, train to use the latest technologies, and find out about the Talking Newspaper.

They offer a 'talk and support' phone service, to help counteract isolation, and arrange social events for those with impaired vision. There is also the chance to join the local VIP bowling club, help out in the charity shop or volunteer to help others experiencing sight loss – the opportunity to be a part of something worthwhile is sometimes very welcome.

A member of staff is based at the Eye Clinic at Southend Hospital, so help and support can be offered exactly where needed.

Southend in Sight receives no government funding and relies entirely on donations. It is a local charity supporting local people and Phoenix Writing Group is proud to support their work with 50% of the proceeds from this anthology.

Also by
Phoenix Writing Group
(Published as WoSWI Writing Group)

Ten Minute Tales

Write On The Coast

A Book For All Seasons

If you have enjoyed our books
please be kind enough to leave a review on
Amazon

Printed in Great Britain
by Amazon

74860079R00113